Forever You

TRADE ME COLLECTION

LAURA N. ANDREWS

HOT TREE PUBLISHING

For information, contact the publisher, Hot Tree Publishing.

www.hottreepublishing.com

Editing: Hot Tree Editing

Formatting: RMGraphx

Cover Designer: Soxational Cover Art

ISBN-10: 1-925448-43-6

ISBN-13: 978-1-925448-43-6

1

MATTHEW

My hands clench around the armrests as my body prepares to spring. I can't help but think of a lion ready to pounce on their prey, only I am the prey—beyond ready to escape. As soon as the seat belt sign above me switches off, I unbuckle my fastening and jump up. I had contemplated the fact that my claustrophobia would be worse on a plane, which is why I've had a fear of flying all my life. For this precise reason, I made it from Seattle to Chicago by Amtrak. Then I finally decided to give it a shot. Now, after just over three hours of flying from Chicago to Brooklyn, I'm tempted to say I should have continued traveling by train. But that's not true; I am ecstatic to finally be here. I've missed my sister so much.

After grabbing my luggage from the overhead compartment, I make my way off the plane as soon as possible, which, given this particular busy flight, seems to take years. When I'm finally walking through J.F.K.

airport, I take a deep breath of relief.

I made it!

Grateful that I've arrived, alive and well, I make my way out of the arrival's area and try to spot my twin sister in the crowd of people. My eyes fall on the other passengers reuniting with their loved ones and it makes me smile. I receive a few appreciative glances and even a couple of double takes from some good-looking ladies. *Sorry, girls, I play for the same team as you.* It takes another moment for me to notice the small, fair-skinned, pretty blonde girl running and waving at me like crazy. "Matty!" she squeals, her legs moving as fast as they can.

I beam at my sister and catch her as she jumps. "Hey, Annie."

Holding on to me tightly, she sighs into my neck. "I've missed you."

"Me too. How long has it been?"

Stepping back, she scrunches her nose. *Damn, it really is like I'm looking in the mirror with her.* "I left home two months ago!"

I shake my head. "That's absurd. We're never going to be apart this long ever again."

"Never," she agrees, leading the way toward the baggage claiming area. "How was the flight?" Her tentative expression tells me she's referring to my claustrophobia. Bless her heart.

"It wasn't fun, but I'm actually grateful. It could have been a lot worse."

Annie frowns. “So you didn’t have a panic attack?” She grabs my bag so I can collect my check-in luggage. Once I have it, we link arms and head out of the airport.

“Only one.”

“Uh-oh.”

I laugh. “It wasn’t too bad.”

“Really? How come?”

“Because when I started to freak out, a flight attendant came to help. He brought over a bag for me to breathe in and kept telling me everything would be okay. It only took me a couple of minutes to calm down.”

“But we always do that. Why was this different?” she asks, amazed.

“He was hot.”

Annie chuckles. “So now I know the cure for my brother’s panic attacks. One dosage of gorgeous-hot-guy to be taken before meals.”

I smirk at her. “Actually, he took a dose of me.”

“What?” she squeals.

“We totally hooked up in the bathroom on the plane.”

“You did not.”

Her scandalized expression makes me laugh. “Yeah, we did. He gave me a nice BJ. Of course, an hour after that, I was uncomfortable again until the plane landed.”

“You’re shameless,” she says with a smile. “Well, I’m sorry you were uncomfortable, but I’m so glad you’re here. I didn’t want to wait any longer.”

“Me too. Are you sure it’s okay that I stay with you though?”

It was clear as soon as Annie moved that I would also be moving to Brooklyn. When she told me at the end of July, she asked me to come with her. I said I needed to start saving some money, but that I would consider it. She'd been living in Brooklyn for about seven weeks when I finally called to tell her I was on my way. Only, that it would take me a few days as I would be taking the Amtrak. It's taken me a little less than a week, but I've made it. Like a lot of twins, we are inseparable.

"Hey!" She whacks my arm, bringing me back to the present. "I wouldn't have encouraged you to come—to *fly*—here if I wasn't seriously okay with it. You're my bro', man." We laugh as she tries to get all gangster on me.

I follow her lead as we make our way to her car. Having been born in Seattle, Washington, I've always wanted to visit New York or Brooklyn before, but this is what happens when you have a pretty bad case of claustrophobia and a fear of flying. With the same desire to head over east as me, Annie moved here for a job soon after she received her master's degree in psychology.

My luggage safe in the trunk of her car, we hop in and drive out of the airport. I let my eyes take in all of the surroundings as I speak. "Hey, so you know how I said I was trying to save?"

"Yep." Annie taps her fingers on the steering wheel to the beat of Beyoncé's "Lemonade."

I let the music flow through my body as I say, "I've

managed to save a couple grand since you left. Added with my original savings I have about seven grand. I was thinking I could buy a crappy car or bike and fix it up myself if I need to."

"Matty, I'll lend you some money so you don't have to buy an old bucket of rust."

"No. Thanks, sis, but no. I'm paying with my own money. Plus, I'll be paying you rent if I'm living with you. You said you knew somewhere I could maybe get a job?"

"Yeah, there are a few places you could look into that are really close to my house. I've asked around a bit too. What are you in the mood for?" She throws me an indulgent smile. Annie knows how many different jobs I've had up until now.

"Maybe some kind of receptionist job?" I ask. "It's been a while since I worked at Mac's garage back home. It'd be cool to be near cars again too."

"So an auto repair shop? Oh, I know just the place!"

Surprised, I turn to her and raise my eyebrows. "You do?"

"Yeah, my friend Stoke. He co-owns Carlson and Stokes Service and Repairs."

"Stoke?" I question. *What kind of name is that?*

"It's his nickname. His actual name is Stokes, Benjamin Stokes."

I mock her with a bad impersonation of Sean Connery. "Bond, James Bond."

Annie scoffs and rolls her eyes. "Anyway, I'll get you the address. I've mentioned you to him, just in case you wanted to work near cars again. So if you head over there tomorrow—or whenever because there's no rush—he'll be expecting you."

"Awesome, thanks."

"No worries. But to say thank you, will you promise to make me a deal?"

"What is it?"

"Nope," she says. "To say a proper thank you to me, you have to promise it before I tell you."

"That's just stupid. Why would I do that?"

"*Please?* For me, please?"

Narrowing my eyes at her puppy-dog expression, I scowl. "You play dirty." Annie turns her face to me just quick enough to stick her bottom lip out. "Oh, all right. What?"

"Say it."

I huff. "I promise to the deal. Now, what is it?"

"Yay!" She claps her hands carefully and then grips the steering wheel again.

I try and fail to hide my smile. "What is it, Annie?"

"You just promised not to pay me rent for at *least* the next three weeks."

"What? No." The idea is preposterous. I'm not living at her place for free.

"Uh-huh, you promised. That's it. The deal has been struck."

"Annie," I whine. "I don't like this idea."

"Nope. It's not an idea. It's a done deal. Think of it as a vacation for all the trouble it took you to get here. I mean really, my need to come here made you come here."

"That doesn't matter. If I were to say I'm moving to Australia, you'd make your way to me eventually."

She shrugs. "Doesn't matter. You're not paying. I mean, I'd be happier if it were at least a month, but I don't want to push it."

"Smart girl."

She scoffs. "You have to be the only person in the world who wants to pay rent."

"You're paying your mortgage off. I'm not going to make it worse for you by living in your house and not paying my way. How about a hundred and fifty a week?"

She shakes her head. "Fifty."

"One twenty."

"Eighty."

"I'm not going below one hundred."

Annie sighs loudly. "Fine! One hundred dollars a week."

"Great. But that doesn't include groceries. And I intend to buy them."

"Only—"

I cut her off. "*All* of them. And any other shopping requirements I think needs doing. *And* I'm going halves with bills."

"You're so annoying," she grumbles.

"Yeah, but you love me."

"Yeah."

We share a smile, and I look out the windshield just as she pulls up to a cute, brown, brick house on the right. Finally, a place where I can stay comfortably for the foreseeable future. Having to stay at a motel in Seattle, travel for a couple of days, then stay at another motel in Chicago, it's nice to know I'll be more settled now.

"What are you thinking about?" Annie asks as she stops the car.

"Just how grateful I am to be here. To know that I don't have to move or leave anytime soon."

"I'm really happy you're here, Matty. You have no idea. Even though I generally work long hours, knowing you'll be here when I come home will make it all the better."

Her words help convince my heart to embrace this new place as it means we will be together after being apart for too long. Perhaps we needed to move away from where we grew up in order to start a new chapter of our lives. Looking at her now, Annie has come so far from her troubled teenaged years. Come to think of it, we both have. But Annie—after going through the grief and behavioral problems as a child who lost their parents too early—she turned her life around when she decided to become a psychologist so she could help people. "Mom and Dad would be so proud of you," I tell her. "You know that, right?"

Her smile is as beautiful as it is sad. "Yeah."

I squeeze her shoulder. "Come on, sis. Time to show me your crib."

Taking my bags out of her trunk and carrying them inside, I feel our excitement in the air.

2

BENJAMIN

"Hey, Stoke! We have a guy in the office wanting a job. What do you want me to do?"

Lifting my head, I pause my movements. "Any qualifications?"

"Don't know. Should I ask?"

"No, that's okay, Luke. I'll be done in a sec." Using a wrench, I tighten the nuts on the new tire I've just placed on a Hyundai Elantra. After polishing the frame with a rag, I stand and wipe my hands. I'm still trying uselessly to clean the grease off of them as I step out of the garage and into the reception area.

A few feet away from the front desk is a kid. A cute kid. He looks to be between sixteen or eighteen years old. His blond locks and blue eyes tell me that girls would call him a "pretty boy." Even as a straight man, I can admit he is pretty. There isn't any other way to describe him really. He notices me and stands up from the chair by the wall. Wearing black skinny jeans, a white top, and a flannel jacket, his only other accessory is the backpack he hangs over one shoulder.

"Hey, kid," I say, holding my hand out. "You the one looking for a job?"

Clasping my hand for a brief shake, the boy frowns and gives me a once-over then takes a step back. "'Kid'? How fucking old do you think I am?"

After raising my hands in surrender, I slip my rag into the back pocket of my jeans. I've obviously offended him. "Woah, hold up. You *are* looking for a job, right?"

"Yes." He tilts his head up to lock eyes with me. *Christ, he's short. I have at least a foot on him.* He must be about five foot four.

"And you're cursing at me?" I ask. "One of the guys you want to work for?"

His eyes widen before running up and down my body. *Is he checking me out?* Suddenly, he clears his throat. "You're Stoke? I mean, Benjamin Stokes?"

The fact that he knows my nickname has me curious. "Yes."

"Ah, sorry. My sister said you'd maybe give me a job."

Understanding hits me. "No shit, you're Annie Price's twin brother? Matthew, isn't it? Jesus, now I get it. I don't know how I didn't make the connection straight away. You're the spitting image of her."

Matthew scoffs. "Only, I'm a man. And it's Matt, by the way."

"Shit, yeah, a *male* version of her." I squint at him. "You're really twenty-six?"

"Yeah." He's annoyed again. His nose scrunches up in a cute way, sort of like Annie's, only hers doesn't make me breathless. "How old did you think I was?"

I chuckle and rub the back of my neck. "I don't know, man, like eighteen?" Obviously, I'm going to pick the oldest guess. Matt still seems perplexed at the idea of looking younger.

"Whatever, man." He shakes his head and his eyes find the door.

Fuck, is he considering leaving?

Suddenly struck by a strong desire to have him stay, I try to apologize. "Look, don't leave. I'm sorry for assuming you were younger. Annie did tell me a few days ago that her twin brother was moving here and might need a job, so I guess here you are. And it's Ben, by the way." Annie Price is my friend and next-door neighbor. Living beside each other for the last two months has allowed us to form a tight bond. Her obsession with certain TV shows definitely helps us get along as well as we do. The fact that she is simply a really cool, laid-back chick who cares about other people also helps. With the same physical features as his sister, both in the face and general body shape, I'm surprised to find myself attracted to Matt. Sure I've been able to appreciate a man's physical appearance in the past, but never to the point of being affected by it. *Why do I find him so appealing?*

"Okay," he says. "And yeah, I'm just staying with her for a while. Until I find a place of my own, anyway. Obviously, I need to find a job real quick so I'm not mooching off her, you know?"

I nod in approval. This guy has a good head on his shoulders. I like that. "That's good. Do you have a résumé with you?"

"Yeah." He pulls his bag forward and reaches in. Handing over a thin file, he hitches the bag onto his shoulder again. I continue to watch him for a moment, taking in the way he moves with way too much interest, before glancing down at the paperwork.

"You've worked in auto repair before?" I ask.

"Yep. My boss taught me a few things, but I was the receptionist, which is what I'm looking to do at the moment."

"Let's see. Since that, you've worked in a grocery store, a salon, and a pharmacy?"

"What can I say, I like to get around." His grin is pure arrogance.

"You move around a lot then?" I ask, trying not to focus on his smile. His pouty lips and straight, white teeth are almost too perfect. Why is he so fucking *pretty*? The strength of my attraction to him is starting to make me uncomfortable.

Matt shrugs. "I guess I'm a free spirit. When one door

closes, another opens."

"Right." My eyes skim the pages and land on the qualifications section. It says that Matthew Price completed his diploma in law enforcement at a community college. The man has dipped his fingers in a lot of different pies. "At the previous garage, what things did you learn?"

He shrugs. "The usual. How to check tire pressure, change engine oil, check and replace spark plugs, change tires."

"Okay cool."

"Yeah, those skills have come in handy a few times," he states lightly with a small smile. Even though he's saying it in a joking manner, there is a serious edge behind it. The fact that he's had car trouble in the past makes me really curious. For some reason, I want to know every detail of each situation that his skills with cars have been useful. My hands clench on his résumé. *Why am I so fascinated by this guy?* The idea that my feelings toward him could be a major distraction and discomfort at work has me questioning my next move. Do I offer him a job or not?

In the end, I consider my friend Annie, and decide to give her brother a chance. Plus, if we had a receptionist, we might be able to take on more clients. "When would you be ready to start?" I ask.

"As soon as I can."

"Tomorrow sound good?"

He grins. "Tomorrow sounds great."

I nod. "Okay. Be here at nine. I can offer you six-hour shifts Monday to Friday with a twenty-minute break. We're open from nine to five, but you're only required to stay until three."

"Awesome. Thanks, man." He reaches forward for another handshake; his gratefulness is written clearly all over his face.

Grasping it in mine, I hold his hand firmly. "You're welcome, Matt. Annie says you're a cool guy and a hard worker."

"My sister's pretty smart, so you should believe everything she says," he quips with a sly smirk.

"She also said you're a shameless flirt and I should keep my eye on you. As I recall, you've mixed business and pleasure in the past."

Matt's eyes narrow. "Yeah well, by smart, I meant smartass."

I laugh. "Be that as it may, I won't have you flirting with any girls coming in here looking for a *fix*."

"Girls have never been a problem." His eyes are like sapphires, blue and hard.

"But you just said—"

"I *am* a flirt. I like to have fun." He shrugs. "But *girls* will not be a problem."

What he's saying finally clicks for me. "Ah." Perhaps he *was* checking me out before. Oddly, the idea excites me.

"Yeah."

I clear my throat. "Okay then. I'll rephrase, 'I won't

have you flirting with any *boys* coming in here looking for a *fix*.'"

"I'm not into boys either."

Okay, now I'm just annoyed. "Well then, what the fuck—"

Matt interrupts me. "I'll hash it out for you. I promise not to flirt with any *men* coming in here looking for a *fix*. How's that?"

The cocky guy that he is winks at me, and instead of slapping that smirk off his face, I shake my head. "Fine. Great. I'll see you tomorrow then."

"My being gay isn't going to be a problem, is it?"

"No," I lie. Who he fucks is his business, but unfortunately for me, I'm even more uncomfortable now. First, I find this guy attractive, and now it turns out he's actually into guys? It makes me feel like there's even more of a possibility of… getting close to him. Which is just fucked. I'm no homophobe, but until now, I was 100 percent straight. The idea that this small, pretty thing of a guy has me questioning that aggravates me.

"Sweet." Matt waves as he walks off toward the front door. *Damn, he has a nice ass.* "Catch you tomorrow, Ben!"

"Nine o'clock sharp!"

"Yes, sir!" He salutes me before shutting the door behind him. Smartass. I don't care how old he is; he still looks young to me. Or too young to be *with* me.

Matt is such a slim, short thing. He seems tiny compared to my wide-framed, six-foot-four build. I assume he's what Annie would call a "twink." When I asked her what a twink was, she'd said a "cute, gay guy, usually slim and short with boyish features." Ever since I met her, she's made her opinion clear that anyone's sexual preference is their own business. She never mentioned Matt being gay, however. No wonder the kid is so arrogant and cocky though. With that hair, his eyes, and those lips, he could be a model. The fucker.

Shaking my head at myself, I head over to the desk to sort out the roster for tomorrow. As tomorrow is Friday, I figure I'll see how the kid handles things and, all going well, I'll write up the roster for the next few weeks tomorrow night, then e-mail it to all the guys.

In the garage, I nod over at my business partner, Ian, to pull him aside and tell him about Matt. Together, we opened our auto service and repair shop a little less than a year ago. We have three other workers besides ourselves. At first, we figured, as business was doing really well, we might cut down on our own hours and hire more men, but it turns out we didn't want to. Life is fucking awesome when you love your job.

"This Matt kid has come at a good time," Ian says. "With the front desk taken care of, maybe Mickey can get that week that he wants off."

This is true. Ever since we opened, we've all just taken turns keeping an eye on the front desk. "Maybe," I reply. "If all goes well."

"Why wouldn't things go well?"

"I don't know. Hey, not that it's any of their business,

but do you think the guys will mind that he's gay?"

"Don't know. Shouldn't though, but I wouldn't put it past them to give him a little shit about it. All part of the bonding process and all."

"Yeah."

"Do *you* mind?"

My eyes snap to Ian's. "No, why?"

Placing his hands on his hips, Ian replies, "You have that uncertain expression on your face."

I shrug. "I don't know. I mean, I'm cool with it. With him. I just feel uncomfortable."

"Uncomfortable how?"

"Are you a homophobe?" I don't think he is, but I want to make sure.

"No."

"Have you… have you ever been tempted to be with a guy?" I can't believe I'm asking what I think I am. But if I was to ask any guy this, it'd be Ian.

"No. Are you offering?" We burst out laughing at the absurdity of it. Ian is happily married with three kids. Plus, at forty-nine years old, he's twenty years my senior.

"I just… He's *pretty*. You'll see when you meet him tomorrow. It confuses me, you know? I've always been attracted to women, and at first glance, I was like, 'yeah okay, this guy is obviously cute,' but he actually is. I don't like it. I mean, I'm straight."

"Wait, you don't like the fact that you think *Matt* is cute, or that you think a *guy* is cute?"

"Both," I grumble.

"How did his sexual preference come up, anyway?" Ian asks.

"His sister said he was a flirt, so I explained that I won't be having any of that with our female customers. He corrected me and said it's the men I need to look out for."

Ian smirks. "Nice."

I scoff. "He's a smartass."

"He's really getting under your skin, huh?"

"Yeah. Let's hope it all goes well for him here anyway, for Annie's sake if anything."

"Oh, this is Annie Price's twin brother?"

"Yeah."

"Well, as her twin, I can see how he's probably pretty then." Ian chuckles.

"Uh-huh." Shaking my head, I tell him I'm going to get back to work. The need to concentrate on something besides the memories of Matt has me getting stuck into it.

The rest of the day flies by and I'm closing up before I know it. It's great having a job that I love because the time doesn't drag at all. I enjoy being a mechanic. Cars have always interested me ever since I was a kid. I received the penchant for car repair from my late grandfather. As a mechanical engineer, he started teaching me things when I was five. Having a doctor and a lawyer as parents, it was no secret that they wanted me to follow in either of their footsteps. When they found out I was leaning more toward the path of my pop, they were shocked. Being as supportive as he was, Pop backed me when I told them I was considering buying a garage with Ian. I just wish he'd lived long enough to see us buy it, but some part of me believes he does see it, wherever he is. Scanning the shop once more, I pull the doors shut and lock everything up, saying good-bye to the others as we all head home.

3

MATTHEW

"Matty!"

I'm in the kitchen cooking dinner when I hear Annie's voice. "I'm in here," I shout back to her.

"What are you doing?"

Glancing up at her as she comes closer, I say, "I'm making us dinner."

She takes a look at my ingredients on the countertop. After settling in yesterday, I noticed the fridge wasn't very well-stocked. When I went to the garage earlier today, I grabbed some groceries on the way back. "Your famous tuna risotto?" she asks excitedly.

"You bet."

"Nice! Want a beer?"

"Yeah, thanks."

"You seem chipper," she muses, tugging her robe tighter around her body. After getting home from work, Annie has been in the shower for a good twenty minutes. I wonder if she's left me any hot water.

Before answering her, I concentrate and finish cutting up the capsicum, celery, and onion, and then open the tuna can. "Well, I got the job you told me about. Went to the garage and your friend Ben wants me to start tomorrow."

"Oh, that's great!" She claps in excitement. "Maybe we could invite Stoke over for dinner to say thanks?"

Ah, maybe not.

"The poor guy will be on his way home from work. He's probably too tired to head over here," I say.

I'm not too sure if I want to see this Ben guy outside of work. The man was right when he called me out on mixing business and pleasure in the past—I did. And the idea of doing that again was unappealing, and yet if it were with Ben.... *Fuck, that man is so hot. With his tanned skin and sinewy muscles, he is definitely my type.* The wide shoulders and thick thighs added to his attractiveness. By memory, he looked like something someone made in a lab, too perfect to be real. His shoulder-length black hair and hazel eyes were the cherries on top. When he called me a kid, it pissed me off, though. In hindsight, he probably thought I was overly defensive, but I didn't want someone as attractive as him thinking I'm too young. Or too young *for him*. He is what, thirtyish? Annie didn't tell me how old he is. Actually, come to think of it, she didn't tell me much at all in regards to him, only that she knew a guy called Stoke who co-owned the shop and could maybe hook me up. *With a job, not him,* I berate myself.

"Oh," Annie says. "Didn't I tell you? He lives next door."

My eyes snap to hers and the knife I'm holding drops into the sink. "What?"

"He's my next-door neighbor. That's how I know him."

"How did you not mention that?" I ask, honestly curious.

She shrugs. "I don't know. More importantly, he's my friend. You know, just like off *Shameless*? Kev and V are like family friends. Sometimes the fact that they're neighbors slips the mind."

The reference to one of our favorite TV shows distracts me for a moment before I take in the information. Shit. This complicates the situation. Not only do I have the hots for my new boss, he's friends with my sister, *and* actually lives in the house beside us. Fortunately, I have a few things going for me. This Ben guy is straight. Plus, he thinks I look young; therefore, there is no way he will be interested in me. That all sounds pretty upsetting, but the thing is, the only guarantee that never fails to turn me off a guy is their disinterest in me. I'm not much of a masochist at all, so I'll be fine. Maybe dinner won't be so bad after all. *Maybe Ben has a hot, gay brother?* Mentally, I groan at myself.

“Oh,” I say, trying to calm my racing heartbeat. “Well, yeah, you could ask him over.”

Suddenly, the loud, clear sound of a motorcycle interrupts what Annie is about to say. “That’ll be him.”

“Ben?”

“Yeah. That’s his Harley.” She gestures me over to the kitchen window. A few houses up along Annie’s suburban street, a beautiful, purring Harley-Davidson comes riding down until it turns into the driveway next door. The man straddling the bike removes his helmet and shakes his hair. Watching Ben slide his sunglasses up onto his head, I’m captivated. As he lifts a jean-covered leg up and over the bike, my eyes follow him as he stands up straight before rolling the bike into his garage. Coming back out, he jogs up his steps then heads into his house. Annie goes over to the back door. “I’m going to invite him for dinner. Be right back.”

“Tell him to stop over in about forty-five minutes. That’s when it’ll be ready.”

“Okay, cool. I might hang out there until then.”

Annie shoves her feet into her Uggs and runs on over. Getting back to the food, I prepare everything so I can cook after my shower. Once that’s done, I head up the stairs and into what will be my room for the next few months at least. After picking out a change of clothes and placing them on my bed, I hop into the shower. I think it’s awesome that Annie and I both have our own bathrooms.

After I’m clean as can be, I throw on my black Adidas

sweats and a gray sweater. Next, I put my own Uggs on. With October starting in a couple of days, the weather is getting colder each night. Thinking of one of my other favorite TV series, *Game of Thrones*, I say to myself in a bad British accent, "Winter is coming." Back downstairs, I cook the rice and begin mixing everything together. Figuring Annie will be bringing Ben over, as she's still not back yet, I set her small dining table for the three of us. About half an hour later, when I hear voices at the door, I'm glad the food is ready.

My sister yells out, "Matty, we're here!"

"Right on time." I turn around, unprepared for the vision that is Benjamin Stokes. By the look of his wet hair, he's just had a shower as well. Trying to keep it cool as my body reacts to him—in the form of my dick rising to the occasion—I wink at him as I realize we're wearing very similar clothes. The only difference really is his Adidas sweats are a navy color. "Great minds, huh?"

"Yeah," he agrees with a deep chuckle.

Fuck. Why does he have to be so goddamn hot?

I clear my throat. "Dinner is ready. I'll just dish it up now. Annie, can you get the drinks?"

She nods over at Ben. "Stoke has us covered."

He holds up a six-pack of Coronas. "I brought supplies."

"Sweet! Thanks, Benjamin."

"You're welcome, Matthew."

As we laugh at the use of our full names, Annie watches the two of us, her eyes going from one to the other. “So, as I was saying,” she says to Ben, “Matt is making his famous tuna risotto. It’s amazing.”

“I’m excited.” His eyes find mine. “Your sister has talked this meal up a lot. So you should know, I have very high expectations.”

I smirk. “Good. So when I surpass them, you’ll be very impressed.”

Watching him smile and shake his head, my attention returns to his hair. *Did he have a shower while Annie was over there?* He must have. The idea that there could be something going on between them never even occurred to me. Of course, now I’m really fucking curious. I start filling the bowls with food. “So, Annie, since you’ve moved here, have you met anyone special? Gone on any dates?” When it comes to my sister and her romantic life, she is the complete opposite to me. While I am confident and sexually active to the point of being cocky and slutty, Annie is the quiet type. However, I know by bringing the subject up, I should be able to figure out whether or not she has a thing for *Stoke* and vice versa.

I doubt I’ll ever call him by that silly name.

As I’d hoped, Annie scoffs. “No. I would have told you if I had.”

I release a sigh of relief. If she had a thing for Ben, she would have blushed and gone silent at my question. “Really? You didn’t tell me about the last guy.”

“That’s because there was no point. We only went on one date and it didn’t go further than that.”

I shrug in response. “Dinner’s up. Come and get it.”

Gesturing to the bowls on the counter, I take mine into the dining room and sit at the table. Ben sits opposite me, which I appreciate because it leaves Annie at the head of the table.

"Why didn't it work out, Pricey?" Ben asks as he looks to Annie.

"I found out he had a girlfriend and he was just looking to see if there were better fish in the sea."

"What an asshole—"

Cutting Ben off, I stare at him. "I'm sorry, 'Pricey'?"

He laughs. "Well, since she gave me a nickname, I gave her one as well."

"Wait, *you* came up with his nickname, Stoke?" I ask my sister.

"Yep!"

"It's caught on too," Ben grumbles with exaggeration. "All the guys at work use it now."

"Come on, it makes total sense!" She gestures wildly with her small hands. "You're a mechanic. You work with cars. Cars need fuel. And you're so hot you'll always *stoke* someone's fire." She ends her speech with a wink. Curious. Although she's teasing and flirting, it's already clear to me that neither of them have a romantic interest in the other. There's no spark there.

After a couple of seconds, we're all laughing our asses off. "Oh, my God, Annie. You're so lame!" I chuckle.

"Oh, shut up!" She grins and stuffs her face with food.

"At least it's not as lame as mine," Ben says to me. "Taking in your last name like she did, I just made it

'Pricey' because I've learned, when it comes to shopping with your sister, she's a brand whore. She only goes for the expensive stuff."

"Someone should write a book about you guys on a shopping trip," I say with a smile. "*The Adventures of Pricey and Stoke!*" Ben's sudden boom of a laugh has my cheeks hurting. It's a good hurt though. It's because I'm smiling too much, and when is that a bad thing? Shaking my head at myself, we all start eating properly.

Ben suddenly exclaims, "Damn! You were right, you cocky bastard. You have definitely exceeded my expectations. I'm not a big fan of tuna, but this risotto is delicious."

"Thank you," I reply quietly. Normally, I would have come up with a decent comeback, but I'm momentarily stumped. Hearing Ben say a word including "cock" with that deep, sexy drawl of his makes me all hot. I can't help but imagine him saying other things like, "Suck my cock," or "ride my cock." Clearing my throat, I knock back a few gulps of my beer.

"So good," Annie adds with a moan of approval.

I mentally pat myself on the back. "Everyone knows, a way to a man's heart is through his stomach. Therefore, knowing how to cook does come in handy."

"You need to teach me," Annie says.

"Now that I'm here, I will."

"Good. Oh, I forgot! I have dessert." She stands. "I'll just take it out of the freezer. It needs to thaw. You guys want another drink?"

"Yeah."

"Yeah, thanks."

Annie runs off to the kitchen.

Ben coughs. "I mean it, Matt, this is great. Who taught you how to cook?"

"Thanks. Our aunty back in Seattle. Although, over time, I've added my own things in there to make it mine."

Ben nods. Looking toward the kitchen, he leans forward over the table. His eyes hold an intense flare. "I'm sorry again about earlier. Calling you a kid and all. Even though I thought you looked younger when I first saw you, it's clear now how mature you are. I guess you just seem so… youthful."

I blink slowly. "That's okay. I know I'm pretty small for my age."

"You mean pretty *and* small," Ben mutters as he leans back into his chair.

Huh? My eyebrows jump up at his words. I must have heard him wrong. "What?"

"Oh, come on. You know you're gorgeous."

My face heats up just as Annie comes in and sits back down. "Matt, you feeling okay? Your face is red."

"Nah, I'm fine. Just caught a little chunk of chili."

"Oh, I didn't realize there was any," she muses.

"There is," I lie.

Ben's grinning at me. The asshole knows I'm lying. He knows I'm fucking blushing because of him. I still can't believe he just called me pretty and gorgeous. *I thought he was straight?* What. The. Fuck?

4

BENJAMIN

Watching Matt both blush and scowl up at me, I decide to help him out a little. I did just call him pretty and gorgeous, which is the reason for his rosy cheeks. He's just too cute, frowning like an angry kitten. "Yeah," I say. "I think I caught some just before. I like it. The chili adds a little spice to it."

Annie shrugs. "I must have missed out. Oh well, I don't mind. I'm not too fond of chili, anyway."

Matt scoffs. "I know. That's why I didn't—" With a kick to his shin, I let him know before he tells the truth, that he didn't put any in the meal. He clears his throat. "That's why I made sure there wasn't any in yours."

"Oh. Thanks, Matty."

Matt gives me a grateful expression as he pushes

his chair back, hooks a leg onto his knee and rubs it. Shit, I kicked him too hard. Checking that his sister isn't looking, I mouth an apology to him. He waves it away with his hand. *God, he's adorable.* "So, what's for dessert then?" he asks, taking a sip of his beer.

Annie grins. "Your favorite!"

"Chocolate Bavarian pie?"

"Yep."

Matt beams. "Nice! Do you happen to have—"

"Coffee? Of course."

"You're awesome."

"I know."

"So humble."

"Says you!"

Watching the two of them interact makes me laugh indulgently. "You guys are a damn tennis match!" They turn to me with identical grins. "You're both so fucking cute." They're cute together, but I realize, I could just watch Matt smiling for hours. The affect he has on me is both surprising and fragile, so much so that I want to cherish it. My attraction is real, palpable, and hell if this gorgeous guy has me questioning everything.

"Oh, be careful," Annie warns me. "If my brother believes for a second that you think he's cute, he'll pounce and probably convince you to sleep with him."

Trying and failing to stop my heart from racing in excitement, I have the sense that I'm grinning like an idiot.

"Excuse me?" Matt blurts out, spilling some of his

beer. The urge to lick up the drops on his chin is almost overwhelming.

Annie shrugs at Matt. "What? Ben is the embodiment of your type when it comes to guys. If he were gay and not your boss, you two would have already shagged."

"'*Shagged?*'" I laugh at her.

Matt explains, "It's from our mom's side. She was British."

"Ah."

He turns to his sister. "And even if it is true, Annie, please stop telling my boss how much of a slut I used to be."

"You still are."

"Shut up."

Wait. What is true? The notion that we would have had sex if I weren't his boss and gay myself? Or that he used to be—and might still be—a slut? Maybe we could work something out at the garage so that Ian is his boss and I'm just a colleague to Matt. That way, if we did want to hook up, things wouldn't be weird at work. I finish off my meal and sit back. "Well, either way, the two of you are adorable." I've surprised myself my embracing the fact that I think Matt is cute and pretty. He has me so… *interested.* No woman has ever captivated me to this extent, so I find myself luxuriating in the fascination I have for him.

Annie smiles. "Thanks, Stoke."

"Thanks, *Ben.*"

My eyes lock with Matt's as I return his smirk. I find

it very intriguing that he insists on calling me by my proper name. More interesting is the fact that I like it. A lot. Annie tells us that she's going to wash the dishes and then serve up dessert. We don't break eye contact as she collects our bowls. "Thanks," we say to her in unison.

"No worries. I'll boil the kettle, as well."

Once she's left, I ask him, "You both drink coffee?"

He frowns. "Yes."

"You should get a coffeemaker," I suggest.

"Oh." He doesn't seem to have considered it. "Yeah. Maybe I should buy us one."

"You should. It's a lot better than instant."

"I'll look into it then, thanks."

"You're welcome."

Matt nods and fidgets for a moment with his beer bottle before taking a deep pull. Wiping his mouth, he says, "I thought you liked women."

My eyes hold his as I tell him the truth. "I do."

"Then *why*, by calling me, 'pretty,' 'cute,' and, 'adorable,' do I get the feeling that you're flirting with me?"

I shrug and take a leap into the unknown. "Maybe I am."

"So you're bi?"

"Up until earlier today, I thought I was completely straight. Turns out, you've caught my attention anyway. You make me feel… uncomfortable." *Among many other things.*

He sits back, furrows his brows, and crosses his arms

over his chest. "Uncomfortable how?"

"You make me curious about things I've never even considered before." Having never been sexually attracted to a guy before, it's odd yearning for these new desires.

"Like what?"

"Like what it's like to kiss a man."

More specifically, to kiss you.

He gasps then captures his bottom lip between his teeth. "Are you saying you want to experiment or some shit?"

Not liking the word, but figuring it's the best way to describe what we'd be doing initially, I ask, "Would you be opposed to it if I said yes?"

"I don't know."

I can appreciate his honesty. "Well. Then, yes. I do want to experiment with you," I admit. "You make me want things I've never wanted before."

Again, Matt seems breathless. "What things do you want?"

With my eyes on his, I pour all of the desires I feel for him into my gaze and speak the truth. "To know what your face looks like when you have an orgasm."

Matt's jaw drops. "I can't believe you just said that." I enjoy his shock as he contemplates my suggestion. Seeing the cocky fucker unsettled pleases me. "You realize, as of tomorrow, you are my boss?"

"Yes." Of course I'd factored that in. He's been on my mind ever since I met him mere hours ago.

Matt uncrosses his arms and takes the last pull of his drink. "That won't work."

"How about I have a word with my partner? We could make him your primary boss. To you, I'll just be another colleague." Ian would be up for that.

His eyebrows lift in surprise. "You've thought about this."

"Yeah, I have."

"I like that."

"You like that I've thought about it?" I clarify.

He nods. "Yeah, preparation is key. The fact that you've thought about it shows you're not going in blind."

"So, you're interested?" I ask, trying not to let my hope make me get ahead of myself.

When he licks his bottom lip, my eyes lock in on his tongue. "Yeah."

Snapping my gaze back up, I smile slowly. "Great."

"You know, when Annie told me about you, she forgot to mention you two are neighbors."

I shrug. "Pricey's not just my neighbor. She's a good friend," I explain. "I realize we haven't known each other long at all, but your sister is cool. Real easy to talk to."

"Yeah, I know. She said that about you. She also said she hardly classifies you as a neighbor. More importantly, you're her friend. I like that too."

Matt stares at me with those sapphire eyes. I wonder what they will look like in the midst of our sexual activities. The vision of those lips of his around my cock has me adjusting myself. "That I'm friends with your sister?" I ask.

"Yeah." He nods. "You must be pretty special to get

her to open up."

I laugh. "Not sure if I did anything special. We bonded over *Game of Thrones* and *Shameless*."

"You like those shows?" Matt asks excitedly.

"I'm probably in the obsessed category," I admit.

He bobs his head solemnly. "So am I."

This is interesting; we have something in common. "Are you up to date with them?"

"Of course."

"Well, Annie and I watch each new episode together. Maybe now, you can join us?" I want him to know that even though we would be "experimenting," I'm not just looking for something physical. The desire to get to know him as a person is as strong as my sexual hunger for him.

Matt gives me a beautiful, wide smile. "That sounds great."

Shifting my leg, my foot accidentally brushes against his. Matt licks his bottom lip at the soft contact. Deciding to see how he reacts, I stroke my foot up and down his leg. I'd removed my shoes soon after walking into Pricey's place. When his breath hitches, I smile. The tingles of pleasure just from this simple contact is surprisingly erotic.

He pushes his chair back just as Annie returns with dessert, and I watch as Matt removes his Uggs and sits forward again. The touch of his foot next to mine causes a light fluttering sensation in my chest. As we eat dessert and drink our coffees, we continue playing footsies under the table. This is the second time that Matt and I have a secret between us. Something just the two of us know. First the chili and now footsies. It's interesting how delighted this makes me feel. For a second, I wonder what the fuck is wrong with me, but then I decide that I don't care.

"Stoke, what time have you told this one to be at work tomorrow?" Annie asks.

"Nine o'clock sharp," I say.

"I can drop you off before work if you like? You'll just be a little early," Annie offers Matt.

"I don't mind walking," he replies.

I make eye contact with him as I trap his foot in between both of mine. "Wait, you walked today?"

"Yeah."

"I'll take you tomorrow," I offer.

"Are you sure?" His foot slips out, only to stroke its way up my leg and onto my seat. In between my thighs. Lightly and carefully, his toes rub my groin.

Oh fuck.

Spreading my knees and lowering my hand beneath the table, I grasp his foot. Pressing it to my cock, I rub myself against him and return his smirk. "Yes, I'm sure."

His eyes grow hooded. "Okay, thanks."

"You ever ride on a Harley before?" I ask huskily.

"No."

"It'll be a first then."

"It will," he replies with a cocked eyebrow.

Through his confident gaze, I know what is going

through his mind, because I'm thinking the same thing. *It will be the first of many firsts for us.* Suddenly, the anticipation to have him on my bike with me is so strong my knee starts bouncing up and down, releasing my eagerness. Matt licks his lips and it makes my hand clench around his foot. *I wonder what it will be like to lick those lips of his.*

5

MATTHEW

Ben's leg bounces up and down softly and quickly. I can feel it with my foot. The foot that is being squeezed against Ben's cock by his hand. *I wonder what has him so on edge.* The very possibility that it could be me has my mouth breaking out into a grin.

I slowly finish off my dessert. "Hey, Annie, thanks for getting this. I haven't had it in a long time."

"You're welcome." She beams up at me.

Ben speaks up. "Yeah, I've never had chocolate Bavarian before. It was, um…" His concentration derails as his attention lingers on my mouth; to be fair, I'm licking the spoon with such purpose. "*Delicious.*" The last word is a deep rumble that makes my dick twitch.

"I'm glad you enjoyed it." Annie picks up our dishes

once again, all except for our mugs. We both take a sip of our coffee as she leaves the room.

Ben clears his throat. "I'm trying to think of an excuse for you to come over to my place."

"Tonight?" I ask. Boy, the man moves quickly.

"Yeah."

"Look." I bite my lip. "I'm all for casual flings, and I'm happy to try this thing with you, but I don't think we should move that quickly."

He chuckles. "I'm not ready to *shag* you yet."

"Then why do you want me to come over?"

Ben shrugs. "I want to kiss you."

"Oh." For a moment, I'm taken aback by the simple, yet appealing desire. Letting my eyes drift toward the kitchen, I try to calm down, but his words have my heart beating loud and fast. *Why am I so anxious?* "Well, um, I—"

Annie suddenly pokes her head into the room and interrupts me. "Matt, I almost forgot. Show Ben that drawing you did of John Snow and Daenerys." Her remark of the sketch I did involving two of my favorite characters in *Game of Thrones* has me wanting to kiss my sister in thanks. She's just given me and Ben the opportunity we need.

"What a great idea!" I reply with way too much enthusiasm. Pulling my foot carefully out of Ben's grip, I stand from the table and gesture for him to follow me. "Come on, Ben. I'll show you." His responding eagerness to follow my lead has me feeling light with joy. I rush up the stairs with him just behind me.

"Fuck," he groans.

I pause and glance over my shoulder. "What?"

It turns out his eyes are focusing on my ass. "Nothing."

"Nothing, huh?"

"Keep moving," Ben orders. He's trying to intimidate me.

"Or what?"

"Or I'll spank that ass of yours."

"Mmm," I tease. "I like this dominant trait you have." Turning back around, I make sure to sway my hips as I take the stairs at a slower pace. I hear him mutter, "Cocky fucker," and it makes me laugh. Opening my door, I wave him in and then stand aside. His tall, wide frame of a body completely takes over my room. It's like my bedroom has suddenly shrunk in size. For a moment, I hesitate. *What do we do now?* Maybe I should ask him. I nod over to my double bed. "You want to sit?"

"Sure." He takes a seat on the end of my bed and hooks a foot underneath his butt. The other remains on the carpet. Copying his movements so that we're a mirror image of each other, I look up at him.

"So," I muse, "you wanted to kiss me?"

"Yes."

"Well, go on then." I know I'm being bossy, but the nerves are getting to me, and I'm not used to being nervous. *Matthew Price does not do nervous!*

Ben sighs. "Just so you know, if the first one sucks, it's because I haven't kissed anyone in a while. And, as you know, never a man."

I nod impatiently. "Noted."

"And also, if it's bad, just let me have another shot, okay? I don't want to leave you with a bad impression."

"I promise to let you keep kissing me until you get the hang of it," I say, urging him to hurry it up.

"Okay, thanks." Ben shifts his butt closer to me and then rests his hand on the mattress, right next to mine. The other hand lifts to my cheek and he holds my face. My eyes have been stuck to his hazel orbs, but now their concentration drifts down to his mouth. When he licks his bottom lip, I do the same. Pulling me in closer by the hand on my cheek, he tilts my head up as he bends his down to meet mine. Taking my bottom lip in between his, Ben's kiss is at first soft and sweet. He lingers on my bottom lip before giving attention to the top one. Licking, nibbling, and sucking, he learns the ins and outs of my mouth. When he sucks on my tongue, I moan. That noise is the turning point. His kiss suddenly changes. Gone is the soft and sweet. Now, his mouth is hungry and demanding. Both of his hands take control and hold my head, cradling it with a firm, gentle touch as he maneuvers it as he pleases. Already, this is the best kiss of my life.

"Ben," I murmur into his mouth. I let my hands reach forward until they grip on to his waist. Digging my fingers into his sweater, I try to lift it up. The desire to feel his skin beneath my fingers is intense. After breaking away from the kiss just long enough to strip off his sweater, Ben returns to me, hungry for my kiss. Taking the initiative and knowing I'm probably moving too fast, I rearrange myself until I am straddling Ben's thighs. I don't try to stop him as his hands lift my sweater off as well. Then, there is a silent moment as we just gaze at each other, our hands and fingers caressing our newly exposed skin. While I'm quite fair like my sister, Ben's flawless skin has a brown, sun-kissed tinge to it. It's absolutely beautiful, and I can't help but stare. "You're so hot," I whisper.

He actually growls at this, a deep purr emanating from his chest. "You know the only thing that kept running around and around in my head when we met today?" he asks, stroking his thumb over my nipple then leaning forward to place a kiss on it.

I whimper. "What?"

"The word 'pretty.' I know you might not like it because it's not manly or masculine, but I don't give a shit." Ben clenches his jaw as he stares into my eyes. "The only way to describe you is pretty. You're absolutely beautiful. To be honest, it pisses me off."

I try to wrap my head around what he's just said as the sensations of his thumb now caressing my other nipple blur my thoughts. "You really think I'm pretty? Why does it piss you off?"

Ben shrugs and grabs my waist in a firm hold. "I guess it's the fact that you proved to me I don't know myself. And at almost thirty years old, I really thought I did."

I lick my top lip. "I don't mind that you think I'm

pretty. Actually, it pleases me that you think that."

Ben smiles. "Good."

Clenching my thighs around his, I lean into him slowly—giving him a chance to stop me—then press my lips against his again. Sliding my tongue into his mouth, now it's my turn to explore him. He tastes just as delicious, but this time I take it in. There's sweetness from the dessert and I detect some coffee as well, along with Ben's own particular flavor. I let my lips drift from his mouth down to his jaw and kiss along it. Hooking my hands loosely over his shoulders, I let my fingers caress the hair at the nape of his neck. "You taste delicious," I say.

He groans. "Jesus. You're killing me."

"Why?"

"Because you keep making me want to break my own personal rules."

"What rules?"

Ben falls back onto my bed, bringing me with him so that I'm still straddling his thighs. "Rule one: never sleep with someone until after the second date. We haven't even been on a date, and I want to fuck you. Rule two: never show them exactly how much you want them. I'm pretty sure you can tell how desperate I am for you."

He wants to fuck me? Oh, dear Lord, give me strength... "At least you know that I want you just as much. So that doesn't make it as bad, does it?"

He ponders this. "Huh, I guess not."

"And this is different. We're not dating, we—well,

you are experimenting. Oh, before you do fuck me though, you should know something."

Ben's eyes lift to mine. "What?"

I stroke his nipples softly. "I don't hide who I am. If there is ever a situation where you're not ready to admit to your feelings or sexual inclination, that's fine. But I am never going into the closet. Never have, never will. I'm out and proud. And I won't hide who I am for anyone. Got it?"

He hooks his arms behind his head and smiles up at me. "Got it." He bends his legs so I slide forward. I squeal quietly until my body stops with my ass directly above his cock. "Now come here," he commands, his finger tapping his lips. Smirking down at him, I obey and press my lips against his. Once again, Ben's kiss grows hungry and my arousal picks up as well. It's amazing how fast this man can turn me on. As we pant into each other's mouths, I know we don't have much time before Annie comes looking for us.

Breaking away, I ask him, "Do you want to make it to second base tonight?"

His eyes widen. "Are you sure?"

Rolling my eyes, I quickly get off him and pull his sweats down. Followed closely behind them are his briefs. Not removing them fully, I leave them hooked onto his ankles.

Wow. "Fuck." Ben's cock is massive. Both the girth and length of it have me licking my lips and swallowing thickly. *I'm definitely going to feel him when he's inside me.*

"Thanks." There is a proud lilt to his voice, but he has every right to be arrogant about this. The man is hung. Wrapping my hand around the base of his dick, I take a firm grip and move my hand up and down a few times, starting him off with a good old hand job. He gasps in pleasure and his fingers clench my bed sheet. When Ben doesn't look too far off from coming, I cover the head of his cock with my mouth. "Oh, God!" He moans loudly as I lick the tip over and over. I flick it in time with my hand's upward motion around his cock. "Matt, baby, I'm going to come."

Encouraged by his words, I finish him off by increasing the speed of all the sensations I'm providing him. So lost in the moment and aroused myself, I'm surprised when I realize I'm straddling one of Ben's thick legs and my hips are rolling. As I'm blowing him, my hips rock into it, my groin seeking any friction it can find. I continue for just a few moments more until Ben jerks beneath me. Swallowing his cum, I make sure he is completely done before letting go of him. I reach my hand into my sweats. Pulling myself out and over the hem of my sweats, I lean forward and jerk myself off fast and hard with the visual of Ben underneath me. His eyes widen when they look up at me. Concentrating on my movements, he watches me grasp my cock. Jerking myself off, I gasp when my orgasm hits me. Leaning up and over him, I aim my cock down and toward Ben's bare chest and stomach. The desire to come all over his exposed flesh finally comes to fruition as I paint him with my white juices, marking him with my pleasure.

With my only warning the sexual flare in Ben's eyes, his hands suddenly grip the back of my thighs as he draws me forward. Leaning his head up and into my groin, he takes the head of my cock into his mouth. Tasting the last few drops of my release, he moans around me. The sight and sensation of it is so erotic, my breath hitches. Fingers falling to his hair as the strength in my legs weaken, I gently lower myself on top of his chest. Ben pushes me a little further down his body until I'm lying on top of him, our lips pressed together. With this kiss, we each taste the other's pleasure and the sensual act has me moaning yet again. God, it feels easy with this man. I mean, I guess sex is generally easy, but with Ben, it's different. It's natural to the point that it's as if we've been together for weeks. The passion he brings out in me is so intense, it's as though it has a mind of its own.

My hands rest on either side of his head, and I question, "What are you doing to me?"

He grins. "Shouldn't I be asking you that?"

"Okay. What are we doing to each other?"

"Well, I believe those were called blow jobs."

I kiss his nose. "You know what I mean." The idea that this is an trial for Ben is all well and good. However, I know just by tonight's activities, there is a high chance that I could develop strong feelings for this man. Our sexual chemistry is ridiculously powerful. I've never had such a strong, passionate connection with someone before.

“Are you referring to the fact that that was possibly the best orgasm I have ever had?” he asks.

I perk up. “It was?”

“Yes.”

Looking down at our chests, I shake my head ruefully. “We’re a fucking mess. Good thing I have a bathroom. Come on.” Extracting myself from Ben and sliding off the bed, I take a moment to appreciate the view of him in my bed. When he stands, that is when I notice the tattoo on his back. Right in the middle and expanding almost all the way to the sides of his waist is the Grim Reaper. With wings on either side of it, the skeletal figure clutches a scythe. It isn’t shaded in at all, only an outline. Deciding that it just looks plain scary, I don’t mention it. In the bathroom, we clean ourselves up and slip our sweaters back on. Although I’m curious about his ink, I brush it off.

“Well, that was interesting,” I say with a chuckle. For me, there’s a need to lighten up the mood. I feel a little off-kilter at the idea that I’ve just made a mistake. *What am I doing, agreeing to let this man try things out with me? Or maybe it’ll be over now? Perhaps he just wanted to see what it’s like to kiss a guy and get off with him?*

“Where are you going?”

I turn back from my bedroom door to face Ben. “What do you mean?”

“I mean, where are you going? You still haven’t shown me that drawing.”

Surprised that he remembered, I wave it off. “You don’t have to look at it.”

Walking over, he leans down and kisses me quickly. “I want to. Show me.”

Still feeling vulnerable at this whole arrangement and the easiness of his kiss, his order ticks me off. “Or what?”

Ben cocks an eyebrow as his hands drop down to grip my ass cheeks. “Or your ass is mine.”

I hate that the contact and his words turn me on. I don’t want to be turned on. I want to be pissed off. “My ass is not yours, you possessive prick. Just because I said yes to experimenting does not make me yours.” He doesn’t have the right to act possessive, not when I’m helping him test out his new desires.

“You’re such a cocky fucker, aren’t you?” He doesn’t let me reply, because his mouth crashes down on mine. After a moment, the kiss ends as quickly as it started. He pulls away and crosses his arms. “Now show me.”

I scowl at him. “I guess the sooner I show you, the sooner you’ll leave.” Ben doesn’t respond as I move over to my bag and reach in for my sketchbook. Flipping to the right page, I begrudgingly hand it over to him.

Ben’s gaze on my drawing is penetrating, I can’t help but watch him as he studies my artwork. My body tenses the longer it takes for him to examine it. His finger lightly strokes the lines and curves of the characters in their almost-kiss positions. “This is amazing, Matt.” His approval is the antidote for my tension. My shoulders drop and I take in a deep breath, thanking him for the compliment. “No, really, it’s spectacular. You should frame it.” I laugh at him and watch as he flips the pages back, glancing at my other drawings. He pauses at my sketch of a phoenix. “Holy crap,” he says. “I don’t remember seeing anything on your resume about going to art school.”

Lifting my shoulder in a shrug, I tell him I didn’t go to one. “This is just a hobby.”

“Matt, you could sell these. They’re *that* good.”

“Thanks.” Retrieving my sketchbook from him, suddenly shy at his attention, I throw it back into my bag and lead the way out of my room. Figuring that what we’re doing is only a casual thing, I find myself hesitant for Ben to get to know me. Or for me to get to know him, like with his tattoo. If what we have is only going to be an test on his part, why should we get to know each other? There’s really no need. *I mean, we won’t even be friends with benefits, will we? Not if it’s all a secret.*

“Are you okay?” he asks.

“Yeah, fine,” I reply.

After saying good-bye to Annie, Ben pauses at the door as I walk him out. “I’ll see you tomorrow then?”

I nod. “Yeah.”

“Okay.” He smiles widely. “Be ready and out front at eight forty-five.”

“All right.”

Ben glances over my shoulder, and when he looks back at me, he quickly pecks me on the lips. “Bye.”

Nothing can stop the smile that forms on my face as he winks at me when he's halfway between Annie's house and his place. However, once he disappears in the night, my smile fades.

What are you doing, Matt?

6

BENJAMIN

The next morning, after I've stuffed my breakfast down my throat, I wait impatiently for the clock to reach an appropriate time to head outside. Another ten minutes until I see Matt again. The very thought makes me smile. Last night had been quite adventurous.

Although I'm not ready to admit that I might be bisexual or gay, I can say with full honesty that what we did in Matt's bedroom was amazing. Just kissing the guy made me hard. Actually, no, scratch that; playing *footsies* with him is what started it. I hadn't done that in years. When he jerked me off and had me in his mouth? Best. Thing. Ever. No girl or woman has succeeded in bringing me such pleasure before. And when Matt came on my chest, marking me with his cum? It was so fucking hot. I have a feeling that, when we do have sex, he might be a bossy bottom. Suddenly I frown. I hope he knows he will be the bottom. I don't think I'll ever let a guy put his dick inside me. It's not so much the act, but the meaning of it. Generally, and especially in the bedroom, I am very dominant.

Finally, it's quarter to nine so I grab my leather jacket, keys, and wallet. I'm locking my door at the same time that Matt heads over. "Hey," I say.

"Morning," he grumbles.

"Rough night?"

"You could say that."

"You go to bed late?" I ask, grabbing the spare helmet and sliding it onto his head.

He nods slowly due to the weight of the headgear. "Yeah. After you left, Annie and I watched a movie, and then we just ended up chatting until really late." I sympathize with him, but I don't tell him why I didn't get much sleep. He doesn't need to know how long it took for me to stop thinking about him last night. Or that my cock had me waking up in the early hours of the morning to finally relieve myself with thoughts of him sitting above me and jerking himself off. Matt waves his hand in front of my face. "You okay?"

"Yeah." I shake my head and swiftly place my own helmet on. "Let's go."

***

The ride to work is interesting. Having Matt on my bike behind me is at first distracting, but once we set off, I'm completely focused. Although every time he adjusts his grip on my waist, it triggers a sensual warmth in my chest. At one traffic light, his hand accidentally brushes my groin and it makes my cock twitch. When I lift his hand higher and his chest vibrates with laughter, I'm no longer sure it was an accident.

Turning into my parking space, I let Matt hop off before me. After resting my bike on its stand, we head in and I introduce Matt to everyone.

"Guys, this here is Matt, our new receptionist. This is Ian, my partner, Luke, Mickey, and Kyle."

Matt waves. "Hi, guys."

The respective men offer their greetings in return.

"Hello, Matt."

"Hey."

"What's up?"

"Hey, man."

I nod to Matt. "Just stay here for a sec while I have a chat with Ian."

Ian gives me an eyebrow raise as he follows me off to the side. "What's up?"

Sighing, I run my hand through my hair and look back at Matt chatting with the guys. At the same time, he looks up and we share a smile. "Look, here's the thing—"

Ian's eyes widen. "Oh, my God."

"What?" I frown.

"You've already started something with him, haven't

you?" he hisses. After a moment of surprise, I nod. "Shit, Stoke. He hasn't even started working here yet."

Wincing, I say, "I know. Look, I was thinking, when it comes to his employment here, maybe you could take on the role of his boss. I think, if what we're doing is going to work, I need him to answer to someone else first, before I'd ever need to step in, you know? What do you think?"

Ian shakes his head. "I hope you know what you're doing."

Crossing my arms over my chest defensively, I ask, "What do you mean?"

"I mean, this kid rocks up—Annie's twin brother no less—and you're already fooling around with him. I just want you to be careful, son. I know you're trying to figure out what you like, but be sure not to hurt him. You've told me Matt is open about who he is."

I pinch the bridge of my nose. "I know, man. I'll be careful. To be honest, the whole experimenting thing is bullshit. I want to date him, Ian. I guess we'll see how it goes. But what do you say about you being his boss while I'm basically a colleague to him?"

Ian sighs. "It sounds like a good idea. I'll show him around the place, help get him settled."

"Thanks, man." Leaving Matt to Ian's capable hands, I get to work on a hatchback I'm in the process of fixing up.

Throughout the day, I make sure to check in with Matt every now and then when I have a spare moment. Each time I ask how he's doing, I find he's handling things well and seems to have a talent in customer service. He even manages to get a smile out of grumpy Mr. Galloway.

"How did you manage that?" Resting my arms on the counter, my breath hitches as Matt leans forward.

"My charms," he replies with a smirk.

"I see. Listen, I won't be able to take you home at the end of each day. I don't finish until closing."

"I know. I'll just walk." He shifts a few pieces of paper around, but I have the sense that he's fidgeting. The idea that I make him nervous warms my heart.

I nod. "You have plans tonight?"

Matt leans even closer. "I don't know, do I?"

As Luke steps into the office, I automatically pull away from Matt and nod at him as a reply.

"Hey, Ben, can I check with you on something?" he asks.

"Yeah, sure." Heading over with Luke, I make a mental note to return to Matt and find out if he wants to come over tonight.

***

Unfortunately, I never get the chance to ask Matt over. After helping Luke diagnose an engine malfunction, I get stuck talking to a customer for over half an hour. By the time I return to the reception desk, Kyle is sitting in—what I will now refer to as—Matt's chair. "Where's Matt?" I ask.

Kyle nods to the clock. "He left at three."

Matt left twenty minutes ago. I'm surprised how hurt I am that he didn't say good-bye before he went home. Shrugging it off, I try to forget about it and figure I'll see him after I finish work.

The next couple of hours go by fast. Locking up and hopping on my bike to head home, I let the rush of the wind wake me up and clear my thoughts. *I should call my mom when I get home and organize a get-together with her and Dad.* The fact that I haven't seen them for a few weeks makes me feel guilty. They live in an apartment in Manhattan on East 95th Street, and it's surprising how hard it is to catch up with them. Our work lives have us too busy and our schedules just haven't matched up lately.

Arriving home, I open the door, dump my stuff down, and pull my phone out of my jacket pocket. I call Mom and the sound of her haughty voice has me smiling. Although she can be stuck-up and sometimes old-fashioned, I know Catherine Stokes loves me deeply. We set up a dinner date for the following Friday night at an Italian restaurant on Lexington Avenue.

"Will it just be you, dear? Or will you bring that lovely Annabeth with you?"

I laugh. Annie hates being called by her full name, but my mother insists on using it. "I don't know, Mom. I could invite her, but her brother has arrived and is staying with her at the moment. Unless I can invite him as well?"

"Oh yes, that's right, her twin brother. Well, that

would be lovely. What was his name again?"

"Matthew."

"Matthew, that's it. Okay, well then, I shall make a booking for the five of us."

"Let me invite them first, Mom. I'll text you as soon as I know if they can make it."

"Well, all right."

"Okay great. I'll speak to you soon. Say hi to Dad for me."

"Will do. Bye."

"Bye."

I jump in the shower then change into more comfortable clothes before heading over to see Matt. Knocking on the front door, I smile in greeting when he opens it. "Hi."

"Hey." Matt crosses his arms over his chest and scowls.

Great, what did I do?

1

MATTHEW

When it was time to leave work, I had hesitated. I'd wondered if maybe I should wait and say good-bye to Ben. But then I'd remembered how he looked when Luke had interrupted us and he'd pulled away from me so quickly, as if he were ashamed to be close to me. The act had pissed me off more than it should have. *He's allowed to keep personal things away from his work colleagues.* It's completely understandable that he doesn't want his employees knowing that he may, in fact, be sexually confused. *So why am I angry at him?*

Now, standing at the door, he's watching me cautiously as I stare back at him. "Matt? What's wrong?"

Not wanting him to know how much his actions hurt me or how childish I'm acting, I try to shrug it off.

"Nothing. What's up?" I step back from the door and head over to the sofa.

He walks in and then shuts the front door. Moving past the single chairs, he takes a seat on the sofa next to me. "Why do I get the feeling something is wrong? Did I do something?"

"It's nothing," I say. "Don't worry about it." Flicking through the channels, I find one of the *Harry Potter* movies starting on TV then put the remote down.

It's clear by Ben's frown that he's confused. "Okay," he finally allows. "So, how was your first day of work?"

I turn to him with genuine appreciation on my face. "It was really good. Thanks again for hiring me. It's nice to work behind a desk again and keep normal work hours. Plus, the guys seem cool."

"You're welcome. Hey, is Annie home?" he asks.

Shaking my head, I explain she called to say she won't be home for at least another hour.

Ben lets his arm rest along the back of the sofa, behind my head. "Maybe we should make the most of our time then?"

For a man who is new to sex when it comes to the male persuasion, Ben is annoyingly confident. I cock my eyebrow at him. "What are you suggesting?"

"Perhaps a replay of last night?"

Taking a moment to consider it, I contemplate the fact that what we are doing is just for fun. Then I think, *what is wrong with a little bit of fun?* Sure, it confuses things a little because he's good friends with my sister and both the co-owner and boss at my new workplace, but at the end of the day, we're adults. *Surely I can avoid allowing any feelings for him to grow.* And even with all of this fooling around, if Ben doesn't have any interest in me beyond this, then that'll ensure I don't either. Decision made, I stand and head for my bedroom. When Ben remains unmoved, I call out, "Are you coming?"

He's up and over to me in a heartbeat. As we walk up the stairs, his hands find my hips as his mouth finds my ear. "The question is, *where* am I coming?"

Shutting my bedroom door behind us, I ask him, "Where do you want to come?"

Ben contemplates this. "I don't know. I want to feel your mouth on me again, but I also really want to do something else."

He has me curious. "What?"

"You know how last night you came on my chest?"

I smile at the memory. "Yes."

"I want to do that." His voice grows deeper. "I want to mark you this time."

"Where?" Suddenly, it's hard for me to breathe. At his silence, I perk up and ask, "Do you want to give me a facial?"

Ben looks bewildered. "What? A facial? I thought we were going to fool around? I mean, I don't do girly things like that."

I give him an unamused expression and scoff. "Putting aside the fact that you just called a perfectly normal pampering activity a 'girly thing,' I'll have you know that isn't what I meant."

"What did you mean by a facial, then?"

"I meant, do you want to come on my face?" I smirk as his jaw drops. "Yes, quite a different thing altogether, isn't it?"

"Uh, yeah." Ben clears his throat. "We could do that, if you want." His voice is husky with need. I get the feeling he hasn't done this before, which would make sense given that he didn't even know what a facial is.

"Okay," I whisper. Placing one pillow above the other, I strip completely naked, sitting down with my butt on the pillows and my back against the headboard. Ben strips and stands beside the bed. "Come on," I say, letting my hands stroke my chest. "Get on top of me."

He groans at my words. Moving carefully, he positions himself kneeling over me, a thick, muscular thigh on either side of me. Sitting on the pillows means I'm at the right height for this to work. My hands stroke his legs as I nuzzle my face in between them. I take in his musky scent, breathing it in deeply because he smells so good, all manly musk with a hint of citrus. Ben gasps as I suck on first one testicle then the other. Licking my way from the base of his cock to the tip, I let my mouth pay attention to the head before resting back on the headboard. Opening my mouth, I let him guide his cock in between my lips. As he rocks in and out, eventually his hands move to my head, taking full control, and finally, he's fucking my mouth.

"That's it," Ben grunts. "Take my cock." Moaning,

I reach my hands up to his ass and squeeze in encouragement. "You like that, Matt? You like it when I fuck your mouth?" I nod in answer then swallow around him. "Oh, fuck." He pulls out and grips himself in his hand. I sit up a little more with both my mouth and eyes slightly open. He gasps. "Matt, I'm going to…."

"Do it, Ben," I demand. "I want you to mark me. Come on my face."

"Oh, Jesus." His hips buck before quick shots of warmth cover my face. Some drops enter my mouth and I lick up anything I can, tasting his salty goodness. No one's cum has ever tasted delicious before Ben. But now, I actually find myself craving it. "Shit, that's so hot."

"What is?" I ask, slowly opening my eyes properly as I lick the tip of his head clean.

"Shooting my load on your face and watching you lick it all up like it's the most delicious thing ever."

"It is." Some part of me wonders if he tastes this good purely because it is Ben.

"Hmm." He ducks his head forward and licks his tongue up my cheek and then from my chin to my lips. "Not too bad."

As his hand grips the nape of my neck, I meet his kiss with a desperation that is still new to me. Starved for his touch, for his kiss, I lose myself in it. I lose myself in *him.* I'm vaguely aware of Ben sliding down and pulling me along with him. Getting off the bed, he heads into the bathroom and brings back a small towel. Returning to my bed, Ben leans down to kiss me again. My face is haphazardly rubbed clean with the towel as we continue to kiss. All of a sudden, he lifts me on top of him so that I'm straddling his thighs just like last night. Only this time, we are both completely naked.

"Oh." At the intimate contact of our groins, I whimper in pleasure.

"Mm…." Ben rests his hands on my hips. "You feel really good on top of me like this." He stares at our dicks close together. "You're hard, Matt."

"No shit, Sherlock."

Ben laughs. "I *like* you."

My heart flutters and I try to force down any excitement. "No you don't. You just appreciate my pretty face and exceptional ability to suck cock."

His fingers clench, digging into my skin. "Cocky fucker."

"Possessive prick," I retort.

"I *do* like you." His hands drift down my legs and then up the inside of my thighs. I shiver as his fingers follow the V lines that the juncture of my legs make.

I try to concentrate on what he is saying. *By "like" does he mean as a friend?* Are we stepping up from experiment partners to friends with benefits? He has me feeling dubious, so I huff at him. "What are you getting at?"

Ben's eyes light up. "I think we should go on a date."

I snap my hand on top of his, halting his movements, and meet his eyes. "What? I thought we were just seeing how things went. That we were just fooling around?"

"Me too. But let's say for argument's sake that I wanted to ask you out on a date. What would you say?"

Resting my hands on his chest, I lower myself onto him, allowing our cocks to slide against each other. "I'd say, if you want that answer, you need to ask me out on a date."

Ben rocks his hips into mine and we both groan at the contact. "Will you, Matthew Price, go out on a date with me?"

Rolling my hips back and forth, I answer against his lips. "Yes."

"Good." He sits up and wraps my legs around his body. "Now, how and where do you want to come?"

The sensual contact we have right now is beyond enjoyable. "Like this," I whisper, stroking the stubble on his cheek.

Ben rearranges us so that he is sitting on the edge of the bed, feet on the carpet. "Are you just going to dry hump me?" he asks. His genuine curiosity has me kissing his lips slowly.

I open my bedside drawer and reach in for the lube. Squirting it in my hand, I spread it over my cock, his cock, and his stomach. "It isn't going to be dry," I murmur huskily.

"Ah," he says. "You're going to *wet* hump me."

"Shut up," I laugh.

"Hey, I'm new to this."

"I know, I like that."

"Do you now?"

"Yes. I like the fact that I'm teaching you things, opening your eyes to all the pleasures of gay sex. I love the fact that I'll be the first guy you fuck." *I want to be the last guy you fuck.*

"Oh, yes, about that…." He catches his breath as I start to rock forward, sliding my cock against him. "Um, I just want you to know, I'm a very dominant person."

His words make me scoff. "I know."

"And I just want it to be clear that I-I probably won't want to… you know."

I nod, letting my eyes droop with the pleasurable sensations. "That's cool. I'm mainly a bottom. I mean, I top on the odd occasion if I really feel like it, but I prefer to be the catcher."

"O-okay."

"Ben?"

He opens his eyes. "Yeah?"

"Is this okay?"

"Yeah, feels really good." He wraps his arms around my body as I quicken my pace, rocking my hips forward and back, over and over. My dick is rock-hard now, so I squeeze myself closer to his body to try to get the right friction. Something is missing though.

"Hey, Ben?"

"Yeah?"

"You know what will help me come?"

"What?" he asks, eager to please. I reach behind me and take his hand off my ass. Drawing his finger into my mouth, I suck on it as my hips continue to rock into him. My eyes find his as I wet his finger with my saliva. He gulps. "You want me to suck your dick?" I shake my head and pull another finger inside in my mouth as well, sucking them together. His eyes widen as they glance from his fingers, down to my cock, and up again. "You want these inside you?" Ben asks, pulling his fingers out of my mouth. I nod, watching him as he processes my desire. He suddenly hooks my legs over his shoulders, stands up, and spins around to flip me onto the bed. I gasp at the hunger in his eyes. My next thought has me grinning in triumph.

I've released the animal within.

8

BENJAMIN

All of a sudden, I am an animal. Wild with desire and craving Matt's pleasure, I feel possessed. I want his orgasm and I want it now. Whatever I have to do to get it, I'll do it. He wants me to fingerfuck him in the ass? I'm his man. He wants me to suck his toes? I'll fucking do it. Either way, I'm going to do him right. The need to see the look on his face when he comes makes me obsessed. Now that I know what he wants, I'm going to make it clear to him that I'm calling the shots. I gaze down at his naked body lying beneath me. "It's a pity we don't have more time. I really want to fuck you." Matt's jaw drops and his cheeks flush. "You want that, don't you? You want me to fuck this ass of yours." I unhook his legs from my shoulders, bring him in closer to me, and then flip him over onto his stomach.

He moans. "Oh, fuck."

"You like it when I'm rough?"

"Yes," he whimpers.

What an interesting development. Testing the waters, I lift my right hand and slap his ass. "Mm!"

"Oh, Matt," I whisper. "You didn't tell me you like having your ass spanked."

"I didn't until now. Besides… y-you didn't ask."

"Hmm, that's true." I spank him again and it earns me a moan. "I wonder if you could come just by my palm spanking you."

"Please," he begs.

"Please what?"

"I need. I need more."

"More what? This?" I slap him harder this time.

"Yes!"

"You're a naughty boy, Matt. So kinky." The fact that he likes this kind of stuff excites me. It opens up a whole new world of fantasies for us to explore together.

"Ben, please. Fuck me."

"I told you, *Matty*, we don't have time. We don't know when Annie will be home. Unless you want that?" I ask. "You want her to come home and hear us up here fucking?"

He moans loudly. "I don't care! Please."

His words and begging tempt me. Slapping his left cheek then his right, I accuse him, "You're like a bitch in heat, aren't you? Desperate for my dick."

"Yes," he admits. *Fuck, that's sexy.* "I want your cock so bad."

"Well, you can't have it."

"Fuck you."

"No, Matt, *I'll* be fucking *you*. Just not tonight."

"Please." I slap him harder than before. His begging is making me lose control. "Ow!"

I growl. "You can beg all you like, but I'm not fucking you tonight."

Matt whimpers and it almost does me in. Grasping his hips, I pull him up until he's on his hands and knees. Picking the towel up from the floor, I chuck it underneath him. I squirt some lube onto his crack then slap both of my hands on his ass and separate his cheeks. I then adjust my position and with a finger, I spread the lube down his crack until it reaches his hole. Matt moans as I press against it. My other hand continues to spank him in different places until his body is shaking. Finally, I push my finger inside.

"Oh!" Sliding it in and out for a few strokes, I watch entranced as his ass rocks into my finger, hungry for it. Leaning down, I lick my tongue along one pink handprint on his left cheek. Sucking on the skin, I leave a nice, small hickey. I start to press another finger inside him as I stand back. Eventually, I'm sliding them both in and out of him. "Ben!" he gasps.

"That feel good, baby?"

I slap his ass, and he moans. "Yes!"

"Good." Reaching forward, I take his cock in my hand

and stroke him a couple of times then let go. Once again, my dick is ready to blow a load. From where I am right now, I have the best visual, and I'm surprised I haven't come already. "You're so hot like this, Matt." My free hand strokes his ass cheeks as I continue to pump my fingers inside him. "On your hands and knees with your ass in the air taking my fingers inside you. You have the hottest ass, baby."

Matt whines. "You should fuck it, then."

I chuckle. "So impatient."

He groans. "You're a fucking tease."

My palm slaps him hard. "I'll fuck you when I want to. But you're going to come for me now." Moving him onto his back yet again, I push his body farther back so that I can kneel on the bed. "Spread your legs." Matt's eyes widen and he suddenly seems shy. He presses his feet into the mattress and opens them a little. "Spread them wider, Matt." When he does, I lift them into the air. "Hold them out like this, okay?"

"Okay," he whispers. Swiftly, I plunge my fingers back inside him. "Oh!" My other hand plays with his cock before I duck down to suck on the head. After a few moments, I start to stroke my dick as well. Getting an idea, I lift my head up, place my dick on one of his thighs and then move his other one down so that it is squished between them. With Matt on his right side and his legs bent on my left, my fingers are still inside him. "Oh yeah," he moans, squeezing his legs together and pushing back onto my fingers. "Thigh-fuck me." Telling him to touch himself, I match the movement of my fingers with the rocking of my hips as I buck into his legs. Matt's fingers stroke the head of my penis and it causes me to growl. I look down at his face as he suddenly gasps. "Ben!"

With my free hand, I hold his legs together and then set a brutal pace with my hips and fingers. Matt pumps his cock faster and faster. His cheeks redden. His mouth is open as he stares up at me. "Come, Matt," I command. "Come now."

"Ah!" His body jerks as it obeys me. Seeing him release himself onto both the towel and his stomach, I slip my fingers out of him. Still pressed together with my dick in between them, I move his legs up and let my dick slide farther down so my balls start slapping against his ass. Holding both of his legs on the left side of my chest, I thrust away. My cock now slides between his inner thighs and over his dick and balls. One arm holds his legs to me tightly while the other rests on his stomach, spreading his cum.

Matt moans. "It's your turn, baby. Come for me." I grunt in reply as I start thrusting faster and faster. "Mark me again, Ben. Come on my stomach."

Growling, I slap his ass cheek just as the waves of pleasure become too much. Riding the high, I pump over and over until I finally reach the point of no return. "Fuck!" Snapping my head back, I moan with each jerk of my hips. I lower my head just in time to see my cum shoot out and watch as it lands on Matt's skin. The sight of both our cum on his stomach is so erotic. I love that

I've marked him again. Letting his legs go gently, I move in between them. Lying down on him with my elbows on either side of his head, I feel our semen mixing together between us.

Suddenly, Matt's mouth attacks mine. I smile into the kiss and lower myself onto him, relaxed and sated. I find it amazing. I've never come that hard in my life, and I've never felt as comfortable as I do right now, lying naked with him. I'm so surprised by these facts that I tell him. His responding smirk is arrogant and hot, and his sleepy eyes make me feel proud; I've done him right.

I nuzzle into his neck. "How was that for you?"

"Really good, especially considering we still haven't fucked yet."

"I'm taking you on at least one date before that."

Matt strokes my nipple. Then he pinches it. "That's for teasing me."

"Oh really? You're at a disadvantage here, baby. I'm the one on top." Matt bites his lip to keep from smiling. Running my hands through his hair, I push it back so I have a clear view of his pretty face. "I like you."

He rolls his eyes. "So you keep saying."

"Do you like me?" For some reason, I need him to.

Matt huffs. "I guess." I cock an eyebrow at him and it makes him smirk. "Yes, *Stoke*, I like you."

"Good." I kiss him softly.

His fingers stroke my biceps. "So, are you going to think up a nickname for me, then?"

I blink in surprise. "You want one?"

He shrugs. "Maybe."

"I have a good one."

"What?"

Gazing into his blue, sapphire eyes, I lean down to whisper into his ear. "*Mine.*"

He laughs. "There you go again, being a possessive prick."

I hum. "Yeah, but I'm *your* possessive prick and you're *my* cocky fucker. Got a problem with that?"

Matt shakes his head and then pulls me down for another kiss. Sliding my tongue into his mouth, I take full control. After a few minutes of this, I suggest we jump in the shower and get cleaned up. Standing, we both wince at our sticky stomachs and then laugh at ourselves. Matt says we should have separate showers just in case Annie comes home. Luckily, we're both dressed, back downstairs, and watching the end of *Harry Potter and the Order of the Phoenix* when she walks through the door at 7:00 p.m.

"Hey, guys!"

We both greet her. "Hey."

She kicks her shoes off. "What are you guys up to?"

"Nothing," Matt replies.

I shrug. "Just watching TV."

"Okay, well, I'm going to heat up some leftover risotto. You guys want some?"

"Yes, please," Matt says.

I nod. "Thanks."

She starts to move forward only to pause and look

back at us on the sofa. “Is everything okay?”

Matt scoffs. “Why wouldn’t everything be okay? Everything’s fine.”

“Yeah,” I agree, glancing at him before looking back at her. “Fine.”

Annie’s eyes suddenly widen and her jaw drops. “Oh, my God. You guys did it, didn’t you?”

“What?” Matt squeals.

“Yes,” I deadpan. “We’re… sort of seeing each other, Pricey. Is that okay?”

Her silence makes me wonder if she’s going to yell at me. In the last couple of months, we’ve become real close. I don’t want me seeing her brother to strain our friendship. I cherish having her as a friend because she’s a laid-back, fun, cool chick. Shaking her head, she smiles. “Of course it’s okay. I’m just… I’m just surprised is all. I didn’t know you were gay or even bi.”

I roll my shoulders to release the tension. “Neither did I, until I met this one.” Reaching for Matt’s hand, I twine my fingers with his. “I know it’s come as a shock, but I’m taking him out on a date tomorrow.”

“Oh, are you now?” Matt turns to me, all attitude. Fortunately, I can tell by his smirk that he’s happy with this idea.

“Yes,” I say.

He holds my eyes for a second before feigning indifference. “Okay.” Forgetting about Pricey being in the room, I lean forward and grasp his bottom lip in between my teeth. He moans into my mouth and shifts his leg over and between mine. By the time we pull away, Annie is gone. "Where are you taking me tomorrow night?" he asks.

I stroke his cheek. "Who said anything about tomorrow night?"

"What do you mean? You said—"

"I said tomorrow. Tomorrow is Saturday. A date can be a breakfast date, can't it?"

He frowns. "I suppose."

"Good," I whisper against his lips as Annie returns. "Because the sooner our date, the sooner I can fuck you."

9

MATTHEW

The next morning, I'm stressed and nervous. These are two things I rarely associate myself with. Normally, dates don't make me this anxious, but today? I'm freaking out. I know Ben honestly thinks I'm pretty and cute, but I've put so much pressure on myself to look really good for breakfast.

"Annie!" I yell.

"What?" She comes into my bedroom. With a gobsmacked expression, she stares at my room. "What happened in here? It looks like a bomb hit it."

I throw my jeans on top of the nearest pile of clothes. "Help me."

My dear sister chuckles at me. "Why do you need help?" I reply to her, but my words are mumbled.

"What?"

Embarrassed, I say it quickly without breath, "I want to look good for Ben."

"Aw! Sweetie! Okay, let's have a look." She rummages through my stuff and immediately chooses an outfit for me. She picks out my light blue bomber jacket, a white T-shirt, khaki pants, and black converse. When I make my way out of the bathroom dressed, she claps and grins. "Perfect!"

"Really?"

"Yes, you look great."

"Thanks." The doorbell rings. "Coming!" I shout. Picking up my wallet, key, and phone, I kiss Annie on the cheek and jog down to the door. Ben stands there looking too good to be true. He's wearing his black leather jacket, a blue shirt, black jeans, and Adidas sneakers. So. Fucking. Hot.

He winks at me. "Hey, gorgeous."

"Hey." I shove my hands into my pockets.

"Are you blushing?"

"Fuck off." I grin, shout out a good-bye to Annie, and shut the door.

"Hey, you're blush only makes you more attractive." I roll my eyes then start to walk off. His hand pulls me back around and into his arms. "Come here." Ben's lips are soft on mine and his tongue tastes like toothpaste.

Pushing him away with a smile, I step back. "So, where are we going?"

He shrugs. "Just a little diner I know."

"Okay cool."

"Come on, let me take you for a *ride*."

I laugh as his eyebrows wiggle. "You're ridiculous."

"Shut up and get on." It takes a little longer to actually get on his bike and get going. Apparently, Ben finds the sight of me wearing a helmet all too distracting and this causes a delay. The ride to the diner is nice; again, the experience of riding with him on his Harley is beyond enjoyable. With my arms wrapped around him, I feel safe on his bike. Ben drives with a sexy confidence and general patience. Curiously, I decide it is the perfect combination of thrilling and relaxing. Riding with him on his bike is one of my new favorite things. His jacket smells of his delicious aftershave. The wind and speed at which we move makes it exciting, and the vibrations from the engine underneath add to the appeal.

Breakfast is a real test of my self-control. When we're in the diner, Ben explains that we're in Brooklyn Heights. The place is cozy and nice, and the food is tasty. But the only thing on my mind is sex. I feel bad because I wanted this to be more than him testing his desires, and now that he's asked me out on a date, sex is all I can think about—when we'll do it, where we'll do it, and how we'll do it. His words from last night have my impatience growing. *"The sooner our date, the sooner I can fuck you."* Ben starts asking general questions as we eat and we end up trading them back and forth. By the time we finish eating and drinking our coffees, we've learned a lot about each other.

Ben tells me his mother is a professor at NYU School of Law and his father is one of three doctors working at a small medical center. They have an apartment in Manhattan. "Are you close?" I ask.

He shrugs. "I mean, I love them and they love me, but we're not really tight. In many ways, I'm very different from my parents."

"How?"

"Let's just say I'm a little more laid-back. I take after my pop, my mom's dad."

I nod. "So they're the snotty, rich type, then?"

He laughs. "Yeah." He wipes his lips clean before asking tentatively, "Can I ask what your parents were like?"

At the mention of them, a smile automatically forms on my face. "They were great. Annie and I got our blond hair from Mom and our blue eyes from Dad. I love how we are clearly the product of both of them. It sort of helps me in a way."

He nods. "Knowing that you have a part of them? That some part of them lives on?"

My eyes lift to his. "Exactly."

"Annie told me it was a car accident."

I sit back in my seat. "Yeah. We were twelve. They'd gone out for dinner one night when we were sleeping over at our cousins' place. On the way home, a drunk driver ran a red light."

"I'm sorry," he says, shaking his head.

"I miss them all the time, but mostly at important

things. Like our birthday, Christmas, the day we both graduated from high school, and the day Annie got her master's degree." For a moment, we are both quiet. Then, I remember his tattoo. "Can I ask, why the Grim Reaper?"

Ben rolls his eyes. "In high school and a while after it, I was sort of in this gang. We were called The Reapers. It was a compulsory condition. You wanted in, you had to get the tattoo. Someday I'll have it changed." Ben lays his hand on top of mine. "Hey, I meant to ask you, how come it took you a while to get here? I remember Annie being excited when you told her you were coming like a week ago." His question leads me to blush and explain the whole claustrophobia-and-fear-of-flying thing. "So, because you were scared of flying, you slowly made your way across the United States to get here?"

"Yeah," I admit self-consciously.

"Wow, that's really cool, Matt." I scoff and he tightens his grip on my hand. "I'm serious. Most people would be like, 'Nah, fuck it. I don't want to fly,' but you wanted to be with your sister, so you made it all the way from Seattle to Brooklyn."

I chuckle. "When I hit Chicago, I did say, 'Fuck it,' and finally hopped on a plane."

"So you faced your fear as well."

The proud lilt of his voice and the impressed expression he's giving me are almost too much, but I decide to embrace them. "I guess." Hearing the chime of my phone, I read out the text Annie just sent me. "Annie just messaged me saying she's leaving now to meet up with work friends. She won't be back until much later tonight."

Ben smirks. "Oh really? Maybe we should head back then. We could go via the liquor store? What do you want to do for lunch?"

His words confuse me. "We're having breakfast."

"Actually," he says, pointing to the empty table, "we both finished eating about two hours ago. It's one o'clock. Plus, by the time we get back, we'll be hungry again. Well, I know *I* will be."

"Shit, I didn't realize how much time had passed."

He winks. "That's what happens when you have great company."

Laughing at his exaggerated, haughty expression, I get my wallet out. "Let's head off then. We could go to a bakery as well, pick up some nice rolls."

Ben motions for me to put my money away, and then says, "That sounds like a plan." From his wallet, he peels out a fifty and leaves it on the table.

"That's a decent tip," I say, impressed with his generosity. "And thank you for paying."

"I asked you out, so it means that I pay."

"Well, it's my turn next time."

As we walk back to his bike, Ben hooks an arm around my shoulder. The warm sensation of his body enveloping mine added with his scent makes my heart beat faster. He speaks into my temple, "So there will be a next time?"

"If I have anything to say about it, definitely."

At his bike, Ben cradles my face and kisses me softly. "Good. I find I'm rather enjoying spending time with you."

"You should show me how much you enjoy me, tonight," I say.

"Oh, I will."

***

Back at Ben's place, I make lunch while he makes the drinks. Well, after that, he just stands and stares at my behind. Fortunately for him, I don't mind the sensual attention. Luckily, it isn't until we are inside that it starts raining heavily, otherwise we would have been soaked on the ride back. Laying a blanket on the living room floor, we prepare an inside picnic and Ben chooses the film *Taken*. After we've eaten, we migrate from the floor to the sofa and snuggle.

Yes, Ben likes to snuggle, and now, so do I.

When the movie finishes, he changes the channel to normal TV. *What now?* I wonder. *Will he make a move, or should I?*

Just then, a finger starts stroking along my arm. We'd both stripped off our jackets when we moved to the couch. Fortunately, snuggling into Ben's chest keeps me toasty warm. My eyes snap to his hand as it curls around my forearm. He runs it softly up my arm, over my shoulder, and eventually places it under my chin. Tilting my head up, he gazes down at me with such heat that I'm instantly hard. I try to subtly adjust my pants, but his eyes snap to the movement. "Matthew?"

I swallow thickly. "Yes?"

"I'm ready to fuck you now."

Again, under normal circumstances or with anyone else, I would ordinarily make some snarky comment or simply laugh at those words. But with Ben, I find myself turned on and impatient. "Okay," I whisper.

Shifting me around until I am straddling him, Ben stands. The man is carrying me as if I weigh nothing.

God, he just has to stare into my eyes and carry me, and then I'm hot and ready for him.

He continues to watch me intently, as he makes his way toward what I assume is his bedroom, and it makes me breathless. By the time we're in his room, it's as though we've done the foreplay. The second he lowers me onto a bed, I start to strip, only for his hands to stop me. "No. I'll be doing that."

I groan in frustration. "Okay, hurry up though."

"You sound impatient," he teases.

"You could say that. I've had sex on my mind all day—more than usual—and it's all your fault."

"My fault?" He starts to undress himself and it distracts me until he snaps his finger with a smirk.

"Yes," I say. "Your fault. First you tease me last night and then you pick me up this morning for our date looking like the sexiest guy I've ever seen. And you know, I've never been jealous of a vehicle before, but this morning on your bike, I kept thinking how lucky it was that you were riding it." Gone is his shirt and socks. Now, all Ben is wearing is his jeans. *Fuck, he's so sexy.*

He flicks the button undone then draws the zipper down. I'm watching him while licking my lips. Suddenly, I squeal as he grabs my ankles and pulls me down the bed so that I'm spread out. "You think I'm the sexiest man you've ever seen?" His voice is husky with need.

"Yes."

"Well, I think you're the *prettiest* guy I've ever seen. You'd give that guy from that One Direction band a run for his money."

The mention of the UK boy band sidetracks me for a minute. "Harry?" I ask.

"No."

"Louis?"

"I don't think so. I'm talking about the blond one."

"You think I look like Niall?" I ask, flattered.

He shakes his head slowly as his fingers undo my pants and pull them down and off. "You're prettier."

I give a nervous laugh. "You realize you don't need to compliment me, right? You have me hook, line, and sinker. We're going to fuck. You have my word for it." With my pants and briefs at my ankles, Ben pinches my exposed ass cheek. "Ow!"

"That's for being smart. Don't ever joke around when I'm telling you how gorgeous you are."

His serious tone has me cautious. "Or what?"

In the next second, Ben has my cock in a sinful grip. "Or I won't let you come tonight."

I sneer. "Fuck off." Before I have time to process it, Ben flips me over until I'm lying on my stomach. Drawing my hips up and pushing my head down, he has me in the doggy style position in two seconds. "What the—"

Slap!

"Ouch!"

"That's for cursing," he explains roughly. "Don't test me, Matt. I'm horny and I want to fuck you, but if you're going to be difficult, this whole thing is going to be delayed. And you don't want me to fuck you without letting you have an orgasm, do you?"

"Who the hell do you think—"

Slap!

I truly mean to growl at him, but it comes out as a moan instead. "Okay."

Both of his hands massage my ass. "Okay, what?"

"I won't joke about that stuff."

"Good boy," Ben says. His praise distracts me though. "Are you going to be a good boy for me, Matt?"

I scoff. "Boy?"

"Yeah," he breathes against my lower back and then kisses it. And just like that, I don't care what he calls me.

"Yes, I'll be good."

"So, before I spanked you last night, no one else spanked you?"

"No."

"I like that." He grabs two handfuls of my ass and holds them out, exposing my crack. "This ass is mine now," Ben growls. "No one else's." I chuckle and my reply is muffled by a pillow. "What?"

"You're such a possessive prick," I say, smirking at him over my shoulder.

He smiles beautifully at me. "Yeah, *your* possessive prick."

I ignore my fluttering heart to agree with him. "And I'm *your* cocky fucker."

His smile fades and his brows draw together. "Yes."

"So you should totally fuck me. Given that this ass is yours." I lift my ass higher and press it back against his groin.

He pushes my ass forward and my head back down before slapping my right cheek. "So impatient." Before I can respond, he uses his hands to spread my legs apart. Sliding my shirt up, he peels it off completely and then stands up. Walking over to his drawer, he pulls out some lube. Then he takes his wallet out of his jeans pocket. The sound of a wrapper has my body stretching in anticipation. I'm finally going to have Ben inside me. I know I only met him two days ago, but ever since I laid eyes on him, I've imagined this moment. At the feel of his fingers stroking down my spine, my cock twitches and my belly tightens.

"You're going to stay still. Okay, baby?"

"Yes."

"I'm going to spank you ten times to get things warmed up."

"Mm."

"Oh, that reminds me. Have you used a butt plug before?"

"*What?*"

"You know, a butt plug."

"I know what it is." I'm sort of scandalized and shocked that he's asking me this. "And yes, I have."

"Good."

He rummages around, and the next thing I know, he's back and standing behind me. He maneuvers me so that my feet are at the end of the bed. A silky, warm finger slides down my crack and to my hole. Pressing against it, Ben slides his digit into me with no resistance. After a few pumps, he adds another finger and starts a scissoring motion. Just when I start to roll back into him, he pulls his fingers out. "No," I whimper.

"Hold still, baby." Ben's voice is deep with arousal. Something else then presses against me and slowly slides inside.

When did he buy a butt plug?

"Mm. Take it in, Matt." My breathing grows harsh and my fingers clench around the bedsheets. I haven't used a butt plug in a while. Relaxing and taking deep breaths, my body eventually lets it all the way in. "Good boy."

Panting, I lift my head to look over my shoulder at him. Eyes widening at the sight of his naked body, I watch as he licks his lips. Bending over me quickly, he kisses me on the lips, his tongue plunging inside and taking my breath away. Hooking an arm around his neck,

I try to make him stay, to pull him on top of me so that I can continue kissing him. However, Ben has other ideas.

Drawing himself back, he tells me to lower my belly but to keep my head and ass up. “That’s it, baby.”

I’m just about to smile when he spanks me. “Oomph.”

“One down,” he says. By his voice, I know he is grinning. With each smack of his hand, the action causes my ass to twitch, which in turn makes the plug inside me send tingles of pleasure all through my body. By the time he reaches nine, I’m blatantly begging for him to fuck me. *Just like last night.* Dammit. I hate how he makes me desperate for him.

“You’re being such a good boy. Last one!” His palm smacks me once more.

“*Ben!*”

“Yeah, baby?”

“Fuck me!” I growl.

“With pleasure.” I hear him opening and closing what I assume to be some lube. When he pulls the plug out suddenly, I gasp, but I have no time to miss it as something else takes its place. I shiver in anticipation as the silky head of his penis penetrates me. I’m a moaning mess as he slides inside me. It’s slow work because he is so big, and I don’t shut up until he is balls deep. I’ve never felt so erotically full before.

“*Ben….*”

He growls and leans over me until his mouth is on my ear. “I know, baby. You feel really good.” He wraps his arms around me and pulls my chest up so that we are both kneeling. He doesn't move inside me as he uses his hands to widen my legs farther apart. Sitting back on his legs he brings me with him.

I am sitting on Ben's cock.

Ben's hands caress my chest, stomach, and legs, avoiding getting too close to my swollen cock. It twitches nonstop as he strokes my body. Almost roughly, his hand quickly snaps my head to the side before pressing his lips to mine in a heated kiss. I slide my fingers into his hair, attempting to pull him closer. When I realize I can't get any closer, I whimper. Slowing the kiss, Ben nibbles and sucks on my lips. Almost simultaneously, we open our eyes. Lips rest against lips as we breathe each other in. And that is when he starts to *move.*

10

BENJAMIN

Releasing my grip on Matt's head but maintaining our lip connection, I place both of my hands on his hips. I begin a slow rocking motion, lifting his ass up as I lower mine then bringing his down as I tilt mine higher. After a few delicious strokes of this, I increase my movements, sliding in and out a little more each time. I've lost the connection with his mouth, but my lips are occupied with his shoulders. *My boy is going to have marks after I'm done.* "You feel good, baby," I murmur. "So warm and tight around my cock."

Matt hums in reply. Eventually, I reach the point where I pull my dick out almost all of the way and then swiftly thrust back in. Matt's loud moan makes me bite my lip. The sound of his pleasure does not help me maintain control. The sensation of being inside him is too good. I'm not going to last long. As my hands are on his hips, Matt loses the strength to keep himself up, falling forward with his hands on the mattress. I continue driving into him over and over. He gasps at the new angle and snaps his head back. *Ah, I must be hitting his prostate.*

He gasps. "Oh, fuuuck!"

Yep, definitely hitting the good spot now.

"Yeah? You like that, baby?"

"Right there!" he gasps. "Harder." Wild with desire, I grant his wish. Gripping his hips, I fuck him like he wants me to. Setting a brutal pace, I'm pounding into him as hard and fast as I can. The sounds of our skin slapping against each other only stoke the fire, and that is before Matt starts incessantly chanting me on. "Oh, oh, oh, oh!" An impulsive need has me slowing down. "No! Don't you dare stop!" Ignoring his shout, I carefully pull out of him and flip him over onto his back. Shuffling closer to him, I force his legs apart with my thighs then hold them out, gripping the back of his legs. He meets my eyes, and by his soft smile, I get the feeling he knows why I changed positions. *Maybe he wants to gaze into my eyes too?* Using the strength and muscles in my hips and legs, I guide my cock to his hole. Once the head is through, I slam into him. "Ah!"

I pause. "You okay?"

"Fuck yes."

"Good boy." I bend forward to place my hands on

the bed. Matt's legs hook over my shoulders. From this position, I can lean down to kiss him. So I do. Matching the movements of my hips, I start to thrust my tongue into his mouth with each push inside his body. With his hands free to roam, Matt grips onto my ass with one of them and then slaps it, urging me on. I quicken my pace even more. His other hand knots itself in my hair and brings me even closer to his mouth. I won't last much longer. Hearing his quiet gasps, I know my boy won't last much longer either.

"Ben…."

"I know, baby," I whisper. Unhooking his legs from my shoulders I run my fingers through his hair to move it out of his face. I stare down at him. "Come for me." With my eyes on his face and my belly grinding over his dick, I feel and see him come. The violent muscle spasms of his orgasm cause a delicious tightening around my cock and it's too much. "Fuck, Matt!" I snap my head back and thrust my hips forward three more times before exploding into the rubber. Staying still as I slowly come down from the high, I eventually pull out of him and wrap the condom in a tissue before throwing it in the bin. Exhausted, I let the hands pulling me, lower me down. After a few seconds, I realize I've collapsed on Matt's small body, cradled between his legs. I start to move off when he stops me.

"No," he whispers. "Stay."

"I'll squash you."

He yawns. "Stay."

Sliding down a little further, I peck him on the lips and then do as he says. I stay right where I am.

***

There's a light pressure on my chest and then a cute huff. It's the quiet giggle that eventually wakes me up. Without opening my eyes, I ask gruffly, "What's funny, chuckles?"

Matt scoffs adorably. "I've been trying to lift you up for five minutes with no success."

Glancing around the room, I realize I must have dozed off. "Sorry, must have had a nap."

"We both did." He smirks up at me. "For at least an hour. Which is why now my legs are frozen up and really uncomfortable."

"Oh, shit." I slowly lift myself up onto my knees. He hisses in pain while reaching for his legs. "Sorry, baby." Rubbing my hands over his thighs, I try to bring back the circulation. "Better?" I ask.

Matt moans in pleasure. "Yes. Feels good."

I watch him close his eyes and lie back, enjoying my manipulations. *God, he's beautiful.* Naked and gorgeous in his post-coital bliss. "I like you, Matt."

He smiles without opening his eyes. "I like you too, Ben."

"Will you spend the night?"

"Yes."

"Good, I wasn't actually going to take no for an answer."

He chuckles. "Didn't think you would." Eventually, I stop massaging him and he asks, "Start the shower?"

"I could carry you."

"No. I think I'll be able to walk."

I laugh as he slowly and cautiously gets to his feet. When he stands and winces, I frown. "Are you okay?"

He lifts his eyes and gives me a shaky smile. "Yeah. You're just bigger than I'm used to." Fuck. *I've hurt him.* I mean, don't get me wrong, I like that he can still feel me, but I don't want my boy in pain. "No, don't frown. I'm fine. Just a little tender."

Still annoyed that I've made him uncomfortable, I step forward and stroke his waist. "I'll go turn the shower on." Before I move away, he pulls me down for a quick kiss.

In the bathroom, I turn the taps and take a moment to gather myself. Sex with Matt is intense. *But who am I kidding?* I knew it would be. Although I enjoyed pounding into him hard and fast, I feel guilty and mad that he's sore now. *Maybe I was too rough on him? Next time I'll be gentle.* There will be a next time, but perhaps not for a while.

Soft, warm hands wrap around my waist. "What are you stressing about?" He rests his head against my back.

I cover his hands with my own. "I was too rough with you. I'm sorry. Next time I'll be gentle." *I'm new to this*, I want to say. I've never fucked someone in the ass before.

Matt pulls away and turns me around to face him. "Hey, I told you. I'm fine. Yes, I'm probably going to feel you tomorrow, but I like that. Don't be sorry. What you just did was… fantastic. It was sexy and hot and intense. It was the best sex of my life." My eyes widen at his words. "So don't go thinking that you did me wrong or that you hurt me, okay? You did me *really* good."

Cradling his face in my hands, I whisper, "It was the best sex of my life too. That was something else I was thinking about just then."

His eyes grow soft and his smile is wide. "Come on." He draws me into the shower and we slowly, meticulously wash each other until we're both completely clean. Showering with Matt is my new favorite thing—apart from riding on my bike with him and being inside him, of course. Rubbing and wiping his slippery, wet skin, I hold him close to me beneath the spray of hot water.

***

It isn't until the next day when Annie, Matt, and I are eating lunch that I finally remember to ask them about dinner next Friday night with my parents. They seem on board with the idea and Annie suggests she drive us all. I offer to drive her car and warn them that they might want to have a few drinks with dinner. It is often the case when socializing with my dear mother and father that people find themselves requiring a pleasant numbing of the brain. I find myself needing it every once and a while. Eventually Annie agrees and it's settled that I'll be the designated driver.

On Monday night, Matt sleeps over. When we're lying in bed after a slower—but no less enjoyable—fuck, he asks me about my folks and whether we should keep things private for now.

"I think that would be best," I say. "I love what we have going at the moment, but I'm still new to this being-with-a-guy thing. I'd like to be more confident in myself before I tell my folks about you."

"You mean, until you come out?" he asks.

I frown. "I'm not… Matt, I'm not gay."

He rolls his eyes. "Fine, bi, whatever."

"I don't think I'm bisexual either."

"So what the fuck are you then?" His smile is cheeky but his words and eyes are serious.

"I don't know," I admit, quietly. "All I know for certain is that, before I met you, I was into girls and then women, and now? I'm interested in you. I mean, I *really* like you. That's all I know. So far, no other guy has piqued my interest, and I have a feeling they never will."

"Okay, you're not heterosexual, you're not homosexual, you're not bisexual…."

I chortle. "I'm *mattysexual*!"

Matt does a face palm. "Oh. My. God. You're such a big dork."

"Yeah," I admit with a shrug.

"But you're *my* dork."

"You got that right."

Just like that, we start fooling around again until our exhausted bodies twine together and we fall asleep in each other's arms.

11

MATTHEW

My first full week living at Annie's is great. By Wednesday, I've fallen into a routine that works for me. Each morning I ride to work with Ben, spend the day answering the phone, booking cars in for service, and ogling my man. Then at 3:00 p.m., I walk home. Annie and I take turns making dinner, and Ben is a guest almost every night. On Thursday night, he comes over and makes us lasagna and it is divine. When he wants to have sex that night in my bed, I complain of a full stomach.

"Will you suck my cock then?" he asks.

Lying on my back and stroking my slightly protruding belly, eventually I yield. "I'm not moving though."

"Then how…?"

"Climb on top of me. Fuck my mouth."

Ben's jaw snaps shut as he relieves himself of his boxers. "God, I'll never tire of hearing you say that."

"Good." I proceed to open my mouth, and while he slides his dick inside, I reach into my briefs and free my own dick, stroking myself in time with his thrusts.

He growls deeply. "I love your mouth." His fingers thread through my hair as he holds my head still. "Open your eyes, baby." Gazing up at him, I watch his face unfold. "You're so fucking pretty. Especially with your mouth wrapped around my cock. You turn me on like no one else. You know that, right?" I nod, and with my free hand, I stroke his thigh. Pouring my desire and utter attraction to him through my gaze and my touch, I try to show him that the feeling is mutual. "You feel the same way?" At my nod, he grins down at me and quickens his pace.

Later, when we're both sated and cleaned up, I bring up the subject of safe sex. I tell Ben that I had my latest check-up a few months ago and suggest that sometime soon we both have all the necessary tests done. When he questions this, I explain that if we're both completely clean—and exclusive—we can eventually have sex bareback. Ben then manages to talk me into having sex. Apparently, just the idea of him being inside me without a rubber has him up and ready again. This time when we come together, his eyes hold mine with such passion, my orgasm is even more intense than ever. That night I fall asleep counting my blessings and praying to whatever deity there is that things don't change. My only request drifting in and around my mind is: *please let me keep him.*

***

Friday at work is hectic. The phone seems to ring nonstop with customers trying to book in or get quotes. The front door is getting more action than a cheap brothel, opening and closing so many times it becomes a background noise. At one point, I lift my eyes as a tall, sharp-looking man with sandy-brown hair walks through and comes up to the counter.

"Hey, I'm here to pick up my Buick."

"Sure thing," I say, glancing through the computer system. "Was it, Mr. Anderson?"

"Yeah, Andrew."

My eyes flash to his. "Your full name is Andrew Anderson?"

He laughs. "Yeah. My parents were cruel when they had me. Having the initials A.A. wasn't fun in high school."

His charm makes me giggle. I bring up his file and see the charges owed. "I'll go back and check, but your car should be ready."

He shakes his head and gestures behind him. "It is. I saw it out front."

"Oh great. So, altogether with the premium service, tires, and tire change, it comes to $648.00."

"All right then." He grins as he passes over a credit card. I grow flustered as he watches me so intently.

He notices my wrist band and cocks an eyebrow at the rainbow colors signifying my gay pride. When his payment goes through and I finally staple the receipt and hand it over, he winks then struts out. I'm typing up a reply e-mail to a tire distributing company when the door opens again. It's Mr. Anderson.

"Oh!" I mentally tell myself off. "I forgot to go get your keys."

"No, it's okay. Kyle gave them to me."

"Ah, good." He continues to stand at the desk facing me. Kyle walks in to check some paperwork beside me. "Can I help you with something else?" I ask Andrew.

"As a matter of fact, yes," he says, stroking his chin. "You want to go out for a drink sometime?"

My eyes widen. *He's gay?* I mean, sure, he's well put together, but nowadays straight men are actually putting in a decent effort into their appearance. I figured he was one of those metrosexual types. "Um, actually—"

"Drew!" a familiar deep voice booms. "How are things?" Spinning my chair around, I watch Ben as he comes out of the garage area and into the spacious office. His grease-covered hands and general rugged appearance has me salivating. *I wonder if I can persuade him into a joint bathroom break.*

I jump at the sudden clap of their hands and the back-slapping hug they do. "Things are well, my friend. How are you doing?"

"Good. Really good."

"I was just asking—" he pauses to look at my name

tag "—*Matthew* out for a drink."

Sort of lost for words at Ben's instant frown, I shake my head and smile. "I'm sorry, but I'm not actually single. I mean, I'm… sort of seeing someone, so I can't. Sorry." Fumbling my way through, I realize a few words into my explanation that I can't actually say I have a boyfriend. *I mean, as much as I want him to be, Ben isn't my boyfriend.* Kyle is still beside me, but he freezes when I admit to seeing someone.

Andrew glances at Ben and his eyes widen before he turns back to me. "Didn't think you would be, but I thought I'd give it a shot." He waits a beat before saying, "Are you sure you're exclusive? Because you could always have a little fun on the side with me if you're not."

Ben steps forward, bumping his chest into Andrew's. "Back the fuck off."

He smirks up at Ben. "You? *You're* who he's seeing?"

"Yeah. So you can forget all of your *fun* ideas with Matthew. He's mine," Ben snarls. The possessiveness in his voice and the territorial way he stands in between me and Andrew has me needing to adjust my jeans. *Such a fucking turn-on.* Wait, what? He just admitted at work that he's seeing me! Not only does a customer know, but Kyle does too. Holy shit!

Andrew laughs, lifting his hands in surrender. "Okay, man, I hear you. I'm sorry for flirting with your boyfriend. Didn't realize you swung that way."

After a moment, Ben exhales slowly then admits,

"Neither did I, Drew, until I met this one."

Andrew—or Drew—glances over his shoulder at me and nods solemnly. "He could turn anyone."

I scoff. "I'm right here, you know. But thanks, I think."

"It was definitely a compliment, cutie." Andrew winks and then laughs as Ben starts to puff his chest up. "I'm going, I'm going! Thanks again for the wonderful service, as always. I'll be back in a year's time for the next one. Be sure to call me though if you're both out on the town."

Ben sighs exasperatedly then grins. "Will do. See you next time, Drew."

"Nice to meet you, Matthew!"

"You too!" I yell back as he walks out. Ben turns around to face me and for a moment the office is silent.

"So, you two are an item then?" Kyle asks.

"Yeah," I say. "We're… seeing each other."

Ben folds his arms over his chest. "Matt's my boyfriend. If anyone here has a problem with it, tell them to come directly to me. Okay?"

Kyle finally nods with a smile. "Good deal, boss." The way he's acting makes it seem as if he had suspicions all along that Ben is gay.

When he leaves the room, I give Ben my best seductive look. "So, *boyfriend*, wanna go make out in the bathroom?"

"Don't tempt me," he groans, leaning forward to peck me on the lips.

I sigh. "I guess we can kiss and jerk each other off

another time then."

Ben moves around the desk and pulls me with him. He starts heading toward the bathroom and my heart leaps with triumph. "This is getting docked off our lunch breaks, so we better make it quick."

"Yes, sir."

***

Driving to Manhattan and navigating Annie's car through the city's busy streets, Ben handles the vehicle with the same confidence and finesse as his Harley. During the ride over the Brooklyn Bridge, Ben announces that he's going to tell his parents that I'm his boyfriend.

I snap my head to him. "What?"

He shrugs. "Earlier today when I told Drew and Kyle that you were my boyfriend, it felt good."

"Aw!" Annie croons in the backseat with a wide smile.

Ben winks at her. "I don't want to wait any longer. I want them to know that you're mine and that you make me happy. Maybe they'll be stoked that I'm in a relationship again. Guaranteed, they'll be surprised that I'm introducing my *boy*friend, but maybe they'll be happy for me."

"So many 'maybes'," I tease. "Who are you trying to convince?"

He scoffs. "Myself."

Annie leans over my headrest and wraps her small

arms around me as she gazes at Ben. "Your parents love you. I'm sure they'll be thrilled that you've met someone who makes you happy."

Ben beams at her and reaches for my hand, holding it the rest of the way.

***

An hour later, dinner is running smoothly. Given that there is delicious food and Ben's parents—although conservative and poised—are very kind, I find myself having a great time. My sister and I have at least six drinks between us, including a few cocktails and some Jack and Cokes. Despite Ben's warning, it isn't his folks that encourage the alcohol consumption; it's the simple fact that I haven't had drinks with my sister in quite a while. Admittedly, by the time dessert is served, I am a little tipsy. Now usually when I drink, I become even more comfortable and confident. When I'm talking to Brandon, Ben's father, and telling him that his son is a decent cook, he cocks an eyebrow.

"He's cooked for you?"

"Yeah," I say. "The other night he made lasagna for me and Annie."

Brandon snaps his head to Ben. "You know how to cook lasagna now?"

Ben looks bashful. "I might have learned recently."

"Ah." Brandon nods his head to my sister with a sly smirk. "Trying to impress someone?"

There's a moment of silence until Ben replies, "Actually, yes, but I wasn't trying to impress Annie." He reaches for my hand then places it on the table with our fingers intertwined. "Mom, Dad, it's very new, but Matt and I have started seeing each other. What I mean is, he's my boyfriend."

His parents' jaws drop and their eyes look like they're about to pop out of their sockets. The sound of my throat clearing seems to snap them out of it. Brandon leans forward and growls, "*What?*"

"Brandon—"

"Quiet, Catherine." Ben's father interrupts his mother with a wave of a hand. "What do you mean he's your boyfriend?"

Ben clears his throat and frowns. "I mean exactly that."

Mrs. Stokes shakes her head. "Benjamin, when… how? Why haven't you told us you're gay before now?"

He sighs at his mother's question. "I didn't know, Mom. I honestly thought I was straight, and even now I don't think I can put a label on what I am. But the thing is, as soon as I met Matt, I was attracted to him. I mean, look at him!" He grins and gives me a sideways glance. I smile back at him. "We just hit it off and… he makes me happy. I wanted you guys to know. You keep asking me to meet someone special, and now I have."

"We meant a special *woman*," Brandon grumbles.

"Nevertheless," Mrs. Stokes says, "I'm glad that you're happy, dear. That's all that matters. And you do seem like a lovely young man."

As she directs this to me, I'm now blushing. "Thank you, Mrs. Stokes."

"It's Catherine, dear. Mrs. Stokes is my mother-in-law."

As she winks at me, I say, "Okay. Thank you, Catherine."

Brandon stands and throws his napkin on the table. "Excuse me, I need to use the mens." Storming off as he is, he narrowly misses bumping into a waiter.

"Don't mind him," Catherine says, trying to diffuse the tension at the table. "He'll just take a little time to get used to the idea."

Annie nods. "It wasn't so much of a surprise for our parents. It's been obvious ever since Matty was six that he prefers guys."

Catherine smiles gently. "Benjamin told me that your parents passed. I'm sorry to hear that. How did they know at six years old?"

I cover my face with my hand as Annie laughs. "Well," she explains, "he kept chasing around all the older boys in the neighborhood asking for their, and I quote, '*hands in marriage*.'"

Catherin giggles. "Oh, that is adorable."

Laughing, I say, "Of course, the minute they started humoring me by saying yes, I organized them into different days of the week. When I had successfully tied down seven husbands, I enjoyed it for a couple of weeks and then got sick of it. I let them all down gently, though." Everyone laughs at the same time that Brandon returns to his seat.

He smiles as if pleased with himself. "Sorry about that." Apprehensive by his sudden jovial mood, I glance at Ben only to see him frown as well.

"Everything okay?" he asks his father.

"Yes. Everything is perfect." His Cheshire smile causes a cold feeling of dread to run down my spine.

12

BENJAMIN

The weeks following the dinner with my parents are interesting. Simply because Matt and I learn more about each other and how our minds work. His sense of humor and general attitude is one of the many things that turn me on. No one makes me laugh and smile like my Matt. Even in the most serious and upsetting situations, he always manages to see the light at the end of the tunnel. Like this morning at work, Ian pulls me aside and tells me how a mystery person called him a few days ago. When they informed him that an employee wasn't comfortable with the workplace romance between me and Matt, Ian got in touch with our company lawyer.

"What did Tony have to say?" I ask, scowling with my arms crossed.

Ian sighs. "He suggested that you end it. To avoid

a claim of sexual harassment, conflict, or in this case favoritism and to protect productivity and morale in the workplace. He said you should break up with him."

"What the fuck? That's not going to happen!" My fists clench as I try to reign in my anger. The question of who exactly is uncomfortable bounces around and around in my head.

"I know, man, and I'm sorry about all of this. I don't know who that fucking caller was. He said he wouldn't expose the employee, but if the situation didn't change, he threatened to make it public knowledge when the claim came through."

"Oh, for shit's sake!"

Suddenly, Matt walks up to us. "Hey, customers in the reception area can hear you shouting. What's going on?"

"I'll take over the desk for a few minutes," Ian offers, bumping Matt's shoulder and giving him a sympathetic smile as he leaves.

"Everything okay?" Matt asks. With a huff, I tell him what Ian had just explained to me. Scrunching his nose up and furrowing his brows, he gives me the cutest frown ever—again, it makes me think of an angry kitten. By the time I finish speaking, I'm pacing the room like a caged lion, trying to relieve the tension coursing through my body. His hands on my chest stop me. "Ben, it's okay."

"How is anything okay? This is bullshit. We are not breaking up!"

"I agree," he says calmly.

"So, what do we do?"

Matt shrugs as if it's obvious. "I quit."

"*What?*"

"I mean, it's been nice working with you and catching a ride with you each morning, but it's for the best. I'll find another job, don't worry."

I huff. "I don't want you to quit."

He smirks. "Neither do I. I love working here. But this will solve the problem and allow us to stay together." Pushing himself up onto his toes, he pulls me down by my shirt until our lips meet in a soft kiss. "I *really* like you, Ben. I want this to work, and if it means not working together, so be it."

Pumping away with increasing speed, my heart skips a beat when he nibbles on my bottom lip. "I really like you too, baby," I whisper into his mouth.

With him giving me his verbal two-week notice, at the end of the day, Matt shows me a poster that he typed up on the computer. It's a hiring notice that states: **POSITION AVAILABLE** for a **NEW RECEPTIONIST**, inquire within. With my kiss of approval, he sticks it to both the pin-up board out in the front and on the reception desk. The other guys had admitted only a few days into Matt's employment that it was great having someone at the desk full-time. When Mickey taps the sign and asks why Matt is quitting, I explain the situation to him and the news gets around. All the guys are really cool about it; they sympathize and regret that he's being forced to leave us. They promise him to keep a look out for any jobs that he could be interested in. The whole situation and the supportive reactions of all the guys leaves me with an uneasy feeling. Did one of our guys actually complain or was the caller some random dickhead trying to cause trouble for me and Matt?

While eating dinner that night at my place, I tell Matt that I love his resilience. He makes a face and laughs at me. "I'm serious," I say. "I love that nothing really fazes you. You just go with the flow, and if there's a problem, you deal with it and move on."

"Is there any other way to live?" he asks.

"Yes. You could have let your anger and frustration eat at you like I started to. But with you there today telling me that everything would fine, that even though you'd get another job, we'd still be together, it helped put my priorities in order and it made me grateful just to have you in my life, never mind at work."

"Yeah well, I love your possessiveness," he says. "I love that you make me feel desirable and owned. That you call me yours every chance you get. Also, I love the fact that you really don't care what people think. In less than a week, you realized you liked a guy and you admitted it to everyone who cares about you without any fear or embarrassment." After that, we start trading compliments.

"I love your eyes," I whisper.

"I love your hair," he murmurs.

"I love your ass."

"I love your cock."

"I love how you work a pencil when you sketch."

"I love how you work a wrench with a car."

"I love… you." As Matt gasps, I realize what just came out of my mouth. I clear my throat. "I do. I love you, Matthew Price."

Jumping up from the table, he strides over to me. I push my chair back and pull him onto my lap. He straddles my legs and cradles my face in his small, soft hands. "I love you too, Benjamin Stokes."

Crashing my lips to his, I kiss him with a desperation I am only now getting used to. "Let's go to bed. I want to make love to you."

"Okay."

Carrying him to my bedroom, I place him on my bed and peel his clothes off nice and slowly. The anticipation to be with him in this way has my heart beating erratically. Once we're both fully naked and I'm lying on top of him, I speak my mind. "You're the most gorgeous person in the world, Matthew Price." His eyes water and I kiss the tears as they fall. Nuzzling my face into his, I place my lips by his ear. "I'm not a religious man, but I thank God every day that you moved in with your sister. When I asked if you would help me test the waters with my newfound desires and you said yes, you changed my life."

He shudders underneath me. "Any gay man would say yes to you."

"But no other person in the world makes me laugh and smile as much as you do. No one turns me on like you do, either."

Matt smiles up at me when I pull back. "You know, I think the only reason I like being spanked is because it's you doing it. I trust you like no one else and it's an aspect of your controlling, dominating personality."

"You like that, huh?"

"Oh yeah."

"Show me."

"Huh?"

I flip our bodies over so that he is on top of me. "I want you to ride me."

His jaw drops, and then he's all about the fast movements. Matt makes quick work of lubricating my cock, pumping me so that I'm fully erect, and preparing himself with his fingers. For a couple of weeks now we've been having sex bare as we were both given the all-clear by our doctors. We moan together as he slowly slides himself on me, gradually taking me all the way in. Having sex without a condom makes it feel even more intimate as it's skin against skin. At first, he starts off slow, rolling his hips with a gentle sway. It isn't long though before I'm slapping his ass and urging him on while he bounces up and down. Just as we're about to come, I grip onto his hips and jerk mine up and into him over and over. Although in hindsight it seems like a normal fucking session for us, it isn't. The fact that we've said the "L" word to each other changes the whole experience entirely.

***

December welcomes us the next morning, Sunday, with a harsh chill in the air. Matt goes next door to invite Annie over to my place for breakfast. I turn the heat up while he's gone and start preparing food. It is when we are all relaxed, laughing and filling our bellies, that my world turns on its axis again.

At the sound of the doorbell, I stand from the table and answer it, wondering who it could possibly be. Grasping the handle, I pull the door open. Standing in front of me is someone I never thought I'd ever see again.

"Jasmine?"

In all her statuesque, long-limbed beauty, my ex-girlfriend beams at me. "Hey, baby, I'm back!"

Behind me, I hear chairs scraping along the floor. "What are you doing here?" I ask her.

"I've come back to you, Benny Boy. Are you going to invite me inside?"

"Who's at the door, baby?" Matt's voice makes me turn around.

"'Baby?'" Jasmine asks mockingly as she saunters inside, past me and over to the twins. "I'm his fiancée. Who are you?"

Matt's horrified expression cuts me so deeply, I correct her with a growl, "*Ex*-fiancée."

"Ex?" She turns back to me. "I don't recall you rescinding your offer of marriage."

I laugh at her in disbelief. "I'm sorry, but you walking out on me and disappearing off the face of the earth, that pretty much sealed the deal that we were over."

"Yeah? Well, when I left, I didn't realize I was pregnant."

"*What?*"

Jasmine shrugs her bony shoulders. "I'm five months along."

"What?" It seems to be the only word I can say at the moment.

"I'm five months pregnant, as you can see." Jasmine separates her cardigan, showing off her swollen belly.

Annie speaks up then. "Hold the phone. You're Ben's ex—the one who disappeared the day after he proposed—and you're only telling him now that you're five months pregnant?"

Reluctantly, Jasmine faces her with a condescending expression. "Yes. Again, who are you?"

My boy pipes up. "Well, my name is Matthew. I live next door with my twin sister here, Annie. Oh, and Ben is my boyfriend."

"Boyfriend? You're gay now?" she asks me.

I move over to Matt to wrap my arms around him, his back to my front. "He's my boyfriend. If that simple fact makes me gay, then yes, I am."

"Never picked you for a poof."

Matt steps forward. "What do you want exactly? Why are you here? Just to insult him?" His protection of me warms my heart.

"Why *are* you here, Jasmine? Surely you couldn't have come all this way expecting that I'd get back with you? Especially considering I'm not available anymore."

"Well, Benny Boy, that's what I was hoping for. Seeing as we're have a baby together and all. I thought we could get married and everything."

"What?"

Matt tries to step away from me, but I don't let him go. "You're here because you want to marry him?"

She huffs. "Well, I don't suppose he has to, given that he has you now. But it would be nice if you had a decent relationship with your daughter." Jasmine directs this to me with a stern gaze.

"You know it's a girl?" I ask before scowling at her. "And of course I'd want a good relationship with my daughter. I can't believe you're only telling me this now. I'm going to be a dad." Matt tightens his hold on my arms around his chest. The contact from him is a comfort I need right now. That Matt can sense this makes me fall even more in love with him.

She watches us and shrugs. "I could have kept it from you, but I'm reaching out." Jasmine turns back for the door.

"Wait!" I step forward, letting go of Matt but grasping his hand in mine. "Do you have an ultrasound photo?"

Jasmine smirks and reaches into her bag. "Here." She hands over the image of the baby within her womb.

"Oh, my God," I murmur.

"You can keep it." Pulling out a pen, Jasmine scribbles on the back of the photo. "That's my new number. Call me if you want to meet up for any updates. Or maybe just to catch up."

And then, just as swiftly as she arrived, hurricane Jasmine disappears. Spinning around to face the twins, my heart breaks at their identical confused expressions. As they encourage me to sit back down at the table, I try to process what just happened. Jasmine has returned and she's pregnant. I'm going to have a daughter. At first my mind screams with the question, *What am I going to do*? But then, what is there to do? There is no way I'm getting back with Jasmine. When we were together I cared for her deeply, so much so that I proposed. But now? I'm in love with Matthew. Nothing will change that. So really, there is no question as to what I'm going to do. Maybe before I met Matt I would have allowed Jasmine to come back into my life and happily taken her back—even if it was only because it was the right thing to do since we're having a kid—but the fact is I did meet Matt. And I love him. The end.

13

MATTHEW

As soon as we sit down after that Jasmine chick left, it becomes clear that Ben is in shock. I don't know the thoughts running around that handsome head of his, but I bet the car that I purchased a couple of weeks ago—an old yet reliable Hyundai Elantra—that he doesn't know what his next move should be. My hand is still in his, and when I try to slip it out, he squeezes it tighter. "Hey," I whisper to him. When he just continues to sit frozen stiff, his eyes gazing at the table, I glance over to see Annie shrug worriedly. Tentatively, not wanting to startle him, I stand from my chair. Hooking my leg up and over his thighs, I straddle him, wrap my arms around his waist, and hug him close.

It takes a few good minutes, but eventually his arms

start to shift. I sigh in relief when he is clearly embracing me too. His arms are vices around my smaller body and he holds me close. “I love you,” he says gruffly in my ear.

I sniffle. “I love you too.”

Threading his fingers in my hair, he brings my head forward. He blinks as he takes in the sight of my face. “Why are you crying?”

“I am?”

“Yeah.”

Annie nods, confirming the statement.

Taking a deep breath, I admit, “I think I was scared. I couldn’t be happier for you right now. You’ve found out you’re going to have a baby girl. But I think I was afraid that you’d leave me and go back to Jasmine.”

Ben growls. “Never.”

“I know,” I say with a smile. “I know that now. Especially because your first words after she left were that you love me.”

“I do. Nothing could make me leave you. Nothing in the world. You’re mine and I’m yours, got it?”

The deeply serious tone in his voice only makes me feel more loved and cherished. I lean forward to kiss him softly. “Got it.”

“Will you come with me? If I meet up with Jasmine, will you join me?”

Nodding slowly, I stroke his hair out of his face. “Of course, if that’s what you want.”

“It is.”

“Okay then.”

“I can’t believe I’m having a daughter.”

“I know. A little surreal, huh?” Getting up, I gesture to Annie and make a move for the door.

“Where are you going?” Ben asks anxiously.

“Remember I told you I wanted to clean my car?” I ask.

“Yeah.”

“Well, how about Annie and I get started on that. We’ll clean and vacuum the inside, and maybe when you’re free, you can help me clean the outside?”

“Free?” he asks, frowning. “I’m free now.”

“I think you should call your parents,” I suggest softly. “Let them know that they’re going to be grandparents.”

“Oh,” he whispers. “Yeah. I should do that. Yeah.”

“Hey,” I say as I step forward in his arms. “I know this is all a bit of a shock, but we’ll handle it together, yeah? Everything is going to be fine. You’re going to be the best dad!” Squeezing him before I let go, I give him a wide smile then head out the door.

When we’re in our driveway, Annie grips my hand. “How are you doing?”

“I’m fine. I’m a little surprised. Okay, scratch that. I’m very surprised. I never thought an ex-fiancée would come back into the picture with a baby, but hey, everything is going to be fine.”

“Keep saying fine and I’ll know who you’re really trying to convince.” She smiles gently as she hugs me to her side.

"I guess, even though I know how Ben and I feel about each other, I'm still a little apprehensive about this news. What if Jasmine persuades him? What if she ends up talking him into the idea of the two of them getting back together? I'll be heartbroken. They must have broken up around the time you moved here, right?"

"Yeah." Annie shakes her head. "She walked out on him like a week before I met him. You know Ben would never do that to you, Matty. You just said it yourself. You know how the both of you feel about each other. Could you leave him?"

"No."

"Then how could he leave you?"

"Maybe he doesn't love me as much as I love him," I suggest. "Maybe he doesn't love me as much as *he* thinks he does."

"He loves you," she tells me sternly. "Stop being silly and stop letting his ex's reappearance, *even with a baby*, let you think otherwise. Yes, it'll be annoying that she's going to have a presence in your life, but she will not replace you. Got it?"

"Yes, ma'am."

"Good! Now, let's get started on your car."

***

About half an hour after we left Ben to call and chat to his parents, he comes sauntering on over. When he reaches me, I let him wrap his big arms around my shoulders. "How'd it go?" I ask him.

"Weird at first."

After snuggling my face into his chest, I lift my eyes to his. "Weird?"

"Yeah." He frowns. Moving us over to the side of Annie's house, he sits down on the porch then places me on his lap. "Mom answered the phone, but as soon as she greeted me, Dad must have snatched the phone from her. I heard them in the background and she was asking why he'd done it, but he just made a joke of it and said he wanted to chat about manly stuff. Then we exchanged pleasantries, and when I asked him to put me on speaker, he flat out refused. He said Mom was busy, so maybe she was, but it just felt weird. And then, when I accepted it and just told him that he's going to be a granddad, you know how he responded?"

"How?"

"He said, *'Oh, well, congratulations, son. Does this mean you're leaving that Matthew fellow and getting back with Jasmine?'*" My eyes watch him scoff and his eyebrows furrow deeply. "I mean, as if!" he growls. "So I told him no. I told him that nothing could make me leave you and there's no way I'm marrying someone I don't love."

I can only nod in reply. For a moment, we continue to sit in silence until I motion for us to go back inside. "Let's not worry about cleaning the outside. It's supposed to rain tonight anyway."

"Okay. Hey, how are you feeling about tomorrow?"

he asks. At the question, I remember that I'm starting my new job the next day as a waiter. Kyle hooked me up with the position since his Uncle Bob owns the restaurant.

I shrug. "Fine."

"You'll do great," he says with a confident nod.

When we're eating dinner that night sans Annie, I ask him, "When will you call Jasmine to catch up?"

His eyes find mine. "Now?"

"Don't see why not," I say. "Maybe get it over with and make a plan?"

Ben follows my advice and calls the number on the back of the photo. As he's waiting for her to pick up, I take a better look at the photo. "Hey, Jasmine?" he asks into the phone. "Yeah, it's me, Ben. Yeah, I'm good. Still shocked, I think." He grabs my hand and holds it in his. "Look, I just wanted to figure out a day that we can just chat about the pregnancy and everything. Thursday? Yeah, that should be fine." He only says the last part at my nod of approval. We both know that he finishes at 5:00 p.m. and I should finish at six p.m. "Can we say six thirty?" He frowns. "You can only do six?"

I lean forward and whisper. "That's fine. I'll be at your place as soon as I can."

Ben nods and sighs. "Yeah, I guess that would be fine. What? No. I just, I was trying to organize it so Matt can be there too. He finishes work at six. Fine, that's fine. Six is fine. Okay, see you then." He hangs up and huffs. "She'd only do six and she's coming to my house."

"That's okay," I try to soothe him. "I might even be at

your place closer to a quarter past."

"I just want you to be there, you know?"

"I know, but it'll be fine and only for about fifteen minutes."

"Yeah."

"Come on." I put the dishes in the sink and pull him upstairs. "Let's lie in bed and watch *Shameless*."

"Okay."

***

The start of the week is smoothly flying past. By Thursday, I think I have a handle on most of my colleagues at Bob's Bistro. Kyle's cousin, Adam, is a fellow waiter and he's awesome. We get on together like two peas in a pod. There are four other waiters and two waitresses. Two of the guys are homophobes. Whenever I mention anything pertaining to my sexuality—namely when I speak to Adam about Ben—they sneer and then walk off. Admittedly, at first it either pissed me off or made me sad, but now I just pity people who are so closed-minded. To live life in a box, not opening yourself up to anything, and just keeping on the straight and narrow, I could never live like that. Therefore, I ignore every huff and every sneer. Because you can't do anything for people who live limited lives; only they themselves can choose to open their eyes.

On my lunch break, I text Ben encouraging words. I tell him that I hope everything goes well tonight and that

I'm sure it will. I remind him that I'm only fifteen minutes away from home, so he won't have to wait long for me. There is a small part of me that feels uncomfortable with the idea of him and Jasmine being alone together. But although I might not know or trust her, I do trust Ben.

By the time six o'clock hits, I have my bag already prepared and I'm racing out the door shouting out my good-byes. The restaurant doesn't close until 9:00 p.m. but my shift is 10:00 a.m. until 6:00 p.m. I'm in my car when I check my phone. There is one missed call from a minute ago at 6:04 p.m. and two text messages. They are all from Ben. The first text was sent at 5:35 p.m. telling me that Jasmine is there and the second one, which was sent ten minutes later explained that she'd brought him some drinks and they were catching up a little on good times. I feel suspicious of her all of a sudden. Why did she bring drinks? What the fuck? What is she up to and why does it sound like he's okay with it? *And what the fuck does he mean by "good times"?*

Driving as fast as I can without breaking any laws, I make it to my driveway ten minutes later. Getting out, I lock my car before heading over to Ben's place. The front door is slightly open. What the hell? "Ben?" I ask. There is quiet music stemming from his bedroom. The car out the front proves to me that Jasmine is still here. Why the fuck would they have music on and in his bedroom no less? Storming through his place, I stop short when I open his bedroom door. Ben is lying on his back, spread eagle on the bed. He has no clothes on and neither does

Jasmine who is straddling his thighs. *What the fuck?*

"Ben?" I finally ask. His only response is a deep moan.

Jasmine smirks over her shoulder. "Oh, hey there. You want to join in?"

"Fuck you," I say to her. From where I am, I can't see Ben's face, so I just yell at him. "I can't believe you would do this, Ben!" Again, he only groans in pleasure and then says my name. "We're through. It's over." I'm tempted to march over there and push her off of him, but she's pregnant and I'm just so disgusted at the whole thing. The fact that they're having sex, but also that they're both completely naked, I don't want to touch or go anywhere near either one of them.

Walking out of his room and out of his house, I numbly make my way over to Annie's. It isn't until I am upstairs and in the shower that I let the tears fall. How could he do this to me? How could he hurt me like this? Once I'm clean and dry, I slip under my sheets and cry myself to sleep.

14

BENJAMIN

When I wake up on Friday morning, I have a splitting headache and a bad case of what-the-fuck-happened-last-night. Sitting up in bed, I slowly recall the events of yesterday. I'd felt wary as last night approached, and at half past five, Jasmine arrived. I can't remember exactly what happened. When she showed up with some drinks and the suggestion to simply drink and catch up, we did. Well, she had juice. Although I wasn't interested in Jasmine herself, I felt the need to remain friendly. Of course, as usual, it was all about Jasmine. She only spoke about herself and only talked about the pregnancy when I persisted with questions. Even then, everything she said seemed flippant. What's confusing is, after the second drink I had, I'd started to feel off and groggy. Jasmine had persuaded me to lie down on my bed while she put on some soothing music. I admit, it did help. The fact that my body was still and relaxed helped ease the pain in my head.

After that, it's all a blur. I can't remember anything after that. I assume Jasmine left and Matt came home to find me passed out. Although, how did I pass out from two drinks? Maybe the pain in my head was a migraine and it knocked me out? Rubbing my eyes, I slowly make my way out of bed and into the shower. Once I am clean, dressed, and caffeinated, I call in to the garage. Speaking to Ian, I tell him that I'm not feeling all that great and won't be in today. He tells me it's fine as we don't have much going on. Seeing it's just after nine, I head over to next door. Annie would have left for work, but Matt will still be home. He doesn't start until ten. Knocking on the door, I wait for it to be opened.

It slowly pulls back to reveal my boyfriend. Or at least he *sort of* resembles my boyfriend. "Matt?" I ask. His hollow cheeks and wide, red eyes have my heart racing. "Baby, what's wrong?"

He scowls at me. "Fuck you, Ben."

My head snaps back in surprise. "Excuse me?"

"How fucking dare you?" He moves forward and pushes my chest. "Get the fuck away from me."

"What?" I'm so confused right now.

"I said to get the fuck away from me. Don't come near me ever again. I don't care what you came here to say. We're over."

"What? How? Why?" I'm stuttering in my panic. "What do you mean we're over? What have I done?" How could he want to end this?

He laughs humorlessly. "Only fucked your ex-fiancée. Sorry, *pregnant* ex-fiancée. No big fucking deal."

"Are you serious?" I growl down at him. "I would never."

"Oh, but you did," he snaps back loudly. "I caught you with my own eyes last night. Lovely visual." Matt sneers at me.

"Whatever you think you saw was wrong." I try with everything I have to remember last night and how he could have mistaken things. There is just no way I would have slept with Jasmine. "I love you, Matthew."

The smack to my face shocks me like nothing ever could. I have never seen Matt's eyes so full of hatred, and I can't believe he just slapped me. "Don't you dare say that to me ever again."

"Matt, I don't know what happened last night. You have to believe me. Jasmine came over and I had like two beers. I don't know why, but I started feeling off and I went to bed."

"Where she proceeded to ride your cock? Yeah, I saw that bit."

I frown, my anger turning to confusion. Matt wouldn't lie about seeing something like that. "No. I would never do that."

"But you did." Matt sighs and turns back into his house. "Leave me alone, Ben. It's over. What's done is done."

Just as he tries to close the door, I hold it open and gaze down at him. “I’m going to find out what happened last night. I’m going to figure out how and why you saw what you did. Because you and me? We’re not over. We’ll never be over. You’re mine and I’m yours. Forever.”

His eyes start to water and it breaks my heart. “Goodbye, Ben.” With a swift pull, he shuts the door.

Going back over to my place, I’m determined to find out what the fuck happened last night with Jasmine.

***

When I finally get a hold of Jasmine Friday afternoon, she tells me on the phone that last night one thing led to another and we ended up having sex. She’d said Matt had walked in on us. I flat out denied that I would do such a thing, but the grim truth of it was that they both kept the same story, that Jasmine and I had sex on my bed and Matt caught us in the act. Paranoia starts to eat at me. I would never do something like this. I would never cheat on Matt. I love him. Nothing could have made me sleep with Jasmine, especially not two fucking drinks. When I glance at the clock, I see that Matt would have been home from work for at least an hour. I make my way over and knock on the door.

What greets me is his twin sister and her fist. Her punch to my nose surprises me so much, I stumble. Saving myself from falling by reaching a hand out for balance, I stand up straight. “Pricey?” I ask tentatively.

"I don't know what Matt told you, but he's wrong."

She's frowning up at me with such hurt and it reminds me painfully of Matt's face. "How could you, Stoke? He loves you."

My fingers knot in my hair. "I love him! That's why I'm not going to give up on this. You're going to invite me in and we're all going to sit down and hash this fucking thing out. Because I don't care what anyone has to say, I didn't cheat on him."

Shaking her head, she leads the way inside. "I must be out of my mind." When I sit down at her table with her, she rubs her face. "He isn't here by the way."

"Why?" I ask. "He finished work over an hour ago."

She shrugs. "I got a text from him just after six saying that he won't be home tonight."

"What? Where is he?"

Annie scowls. "Not that it's any of your business, but apparently he's staying over at someone's house. A work friend."

I try to gather myself. "Okay. I know this looks really bad, but hear me out. I don't remember much of anything last night…" I explain to her how I can only recall Jasmine arriving alone, having a chat and a couple of drinks, and then nothing more. "She said we got together and Matt said he walked in on us, but I don't remember any of it! The last thing I remember is falling asleep on my bed."

"Well," she says, "it does look really bad, Stoke. I don't know what to say."

I implore her with my eyes. “I love your brother so much. I would never do this to him.”

“I wouldn’t have thought so.” She plays with her fingers.

I shake my head. “I feel like I’ve lost all trust from both of you. I know it seems really shady, but neither of you are willing to believe me when I say I didn’t do this. Why?”

Her eyes snap to mine. “Because you were caught red-handed. What would you think if you walked in on someone fucking Matt?”

“But we weren’t! We can’t have been. You don’t understand. I would have been passed out! I don’t remember anything!”

“Apparently you were moaning in pleasure. That’s what Matt said.”

Letting my head fall into my hands, I wipe my eyes when they start to water. “I don’t know what happened, Pricey. I really don’t. But I know in myself that I would never have done this willingly.”

Her eyes flash. “Never, huh?”

“Never.”

Suddenly, she’s up and on the move. “Come on, then. Let’s just see.”

I frown at her. “I’m confused. What are we going to see?”

“Do you think there’s the slightest chance that Jasmine spiked your drink?” Her question surprises me so much, I’m speechless. “Maybe she didn’t, but I think we should go get you tested. Just to see. If what you say is right, if you honestly wouldn't have done it willingly, then perhaps you did it *un*willingly."

Moving quickly, we gather our things and jump into her car on the way to the closest hospital. The very idea that I could have been drugged shocks me. The fact that this whole thing could make me lose Matt has me fuming with rage.

***

A couple of hours later, my toxicology report comes back. In my urine I had traces of Rohypnol, which is the drug most commonly used as a date-rape drug, also known as roofies. To say I'm in a daze after finding out that piece of information is an understatement. Annie hugs me firmly once she hears the news and then sorts everything out. She speaks to the doctors and organizes an STD check for me. She makes sure everything is paid for and taken care of. It is just before 11:00 p.m. when we're back at Annie's place. She asks whether I want her to call my mom or dad to tell them what's going on.

"No," I answer eventually. "I need to find out why she did it. I don't really want to take legal action. I just want to know why."

She nods, and when my phone rings, she passes it over to me. My voice is weak when I answer it. "Hello?"

"Ben? Are you okay? You don't sound too good." It's my buddy Drew.

"Hey, man," I say. "I've been better, that's for sure. What's up?"

He chuckles. "Just thought you'd want to know that your boy is out on the town."

"What?"

"I was just out clubbing with my friends when I turned around and saw one of my friends sucking face with your boyfriend. I hate to tell you this, but he sure is getting around."

"*What?*"

Drew's voice grows hesitant at my furious tone. "Ah, yeah. I've seen him kissing a lot of different guys here. He's acting like he's single. Is he?"

"No."

"Right. Didn't think so. You better get down here then. I managed to pull my friend away but I have a feeling the next guy that catches his eye is going to be taking him home."

"For fuck's sake. Don't let him leave!" I yell into the phone. "Where are you?" Once he tells me which club in Manhattan he's at, I hang up and stand. "I need to borrow your car."

Annie nods. "What's happening?"

I roll my shoulders. "Matt is out clubbing and apparently thinks he's single."

"I could come with you?" she offers.

"No, thanks. I need to do this on my own."

She smiles and rubs my arm. "I'm sorry I didn't believe you, Stoke. Bring our boy home."

15

MATTHEW

The music is pumping and I'm having a great time. When we were at Adam's place a couple of hours ago and he suggested we go out clubbing, at first I was against it. Now, I'm so glad he managed to persuade me into coming. He knew I was down all day at work, figured this was just what I needed and he was right. The place is great, the music is great, the drinks are great, and the hot guys are fantastic. *The best distraction there is*. Sure, I find myself constantly thinking about Ben, but I do all that I can to forget about him. Adam is off getting us another couple of drinks each when strong arms wrap around my hips and bring me in close to a warm, delicious body. I say delicious because we fit so well together and he smells absolutely divine. He smells so much like Ben. My eyes snap open and I turn around. It *is* Ben. He's here!

"What are you doing here?" I slur.

"I'm here to get you and bring you home."

"Fuck off." I make it two steps before I stumble. Ben tries to help me, but I jump away from him. "Get your hands off me."

"Matt, you need to come with me," he pleads.

"Why should I?" The image of him and Jasmine naked together will always haunt me.

"Because I need to explain what happened last night."

"I already know what happened."

"No, you don't!" he shouts.

Shoving him backward, I slowly make my way to the bar and find Adam. Taking the drink he offers me, I gulp it down in one go. Adam laughs. "That wasn't water."

Suddenly, Ben has Adam's shirt collar in his fist. "Back the fuck off."

"Ben!" I shout. "Let go of him."

"Why? You're mine." His eyes are crazed as he looks down at me. The possessive heat in them succeeds in sobering me up a little.

"No, I'm not yours. But this is Adam, my boss's son and Kyle's cousin. Let him go, now!"

Snapping himself out of it, he lets go of Adam's shirt. "Sorry."

"It's okay," he replies. "You must be Ben. I've heard about you."

Ben huffs. "Only bad, I presume? Pity this one here

doesn't have all of the information." He's gesturing to me and it makes me scoff. "What? So you knew I was drugged last night?" Ben smirks as my jaw drops. *Drugged?* "Yeah, I didn't think so. Let's go."

Apologizing to Adam, I tell him I'll call him as Ben drags me out of the club. Even though the cool air wakes me up a little, the anger comes back full force. "How dare you come here and ruin my night!"

Ben gazes back at me with an unamused expression. "Cut the shit, Matt. Get in." He stops short at the car. Annie's car.

"Why do you have my sister's car?" I ask.

"She lent it to me. You know, after we went to the hospital and figured out that Jasmine drugged me last night."

"Just so you know, I don't believe a word coming out of your mouth. I'm just coming because I'm tired." I slip into the passenger seat and everything goes dark before I have the chance to buckle my seat belt. The only other time I open my eyes is when there's a cease of motion and I'm being lifted.

Ben's voice in my ear settles me completely. "Shh, baby. We're home now. Go back to sleep."

***

The next morning, I wake up groggy and with a bad headache. Cautiously, I stretch my body and realize I must be in Ben's bed. My bed doesn't allow for such room. Opening my eyes, my assumption is proven correct when I glance around his bedroom. God, to think of the last time I saw this room makes me want to vomit. No, I actually need to vomit. Running into his bathroom, I just make it to the toilet in time as last night's alcohol consumption makes a reappearance.

"Hey, baby," I hear him say behind me. "You doing okay?" His hands rub my back and he passes me over some toilet paper to wipe my mouth. Eventually I stand up. He hands over his spare toothbrush and the toothpaste. Our eyes meet in his bathroom mirror. "We need to talk. To discuss things," he says seriously. "But that can wait a few minutes. Have a shower with me?" I can only nod; I don't trust myself not to spew as soon as I open my mouth to talk. As I clean my mouth out, he runs the shower. Moving slowly and cautiously, I strip and join him in the shower. It isn't until he starts to lather up the soap and wash my body that I realize I'm crying. Instinctively, I duck my head and this makes him lift it. Meeting my eyes, Ben kisses my tears away and then presses his lips to mine. "We'll get through this," he says. "I love you, Matthew."

"I love you too," I whisper, not really knowing where we stand.

Ben takes such good care of me. Washing me, drying me, and then dressing me, he's amazing, but I feel like an invalid, and it only makes more tears run down my cheeks. "Hey, stop this," Ben admonishes. He wipes under my eyes with his thumbs. "No more tears."

"What's going on with us?" I ask. He moves me back to his bed and slides underneath the covers with me.

"I need to tell you about what you think you saw the other night." His words make me groan into his chest. "No," he says. "Listen to me. When Jasmine came over and she suggested we just have a couple of drinks, I thought, 'Why not?' Hoping she would explain why she walked out on me after I proposed to her."

"How long ago was this?"

"A couple of months before I met you," he says. "After she left, it was only a week later that Annie moved in next door. A godsend that woman was. Through her easy, friendly presence and watching TV, she got me through the worst of it. But surprisingly, it didn't take me very long to get over Jasmine. Once she was gone, I was able to think more about myself and spend time on things I wanted to do."

"So the fact that she is five months pregnant…"

Ben nods. "It means she would have fallen pregnant when we were together and unless she cheated, the baby is mine."

"Fuck. You think she could just be claiming that you're the father?" I can't believe this chick.

Ben shakes his head. "Who knows? Of course, Jasmine only talked about herself and how successful a model she is these days, even pregnant. After my second drink though, I started to feel off and she took me to bed. She said she'd put on some soothing music. It worked.

As soon as my head hit the pillow, I felt loads better. Exhausted, but better. When I told the whole story, or the only parts I could remember of it, to Annie, she suggested we get my toxicology levels tested. Turns out that Jasmine spiked one of my drinks with Rohypnol."

"What?" I vaguely remember him saying something about being drugged in the club last night, but now I'm actually sober. "The bitch actually drugged you?"

He nods slowly. "Yeah."

"That fucking whore." I'm so furious I think I would put aside my dislike of hitting girls if she were in front of me right now and not pregnant. I want to bitch-slap her so hard her face concaves. "She's doing time," I say. "You know she could get like, ten years for drugging you? Added to that, if she did actually rape you, it'd be more."

He shakes his head. "I don't really care about the legality of it. I don't think she fucked me. I think she just sat on top of me just so you could see it. I just want to know why. Why she did it."

"To get in between us? To break us up?" I suggest.

"But why? What does she get out of it?"

"The sick thrill?"

Ben shakes his head. "She wouldn't do something like this without getting something in return."

"You think someone else is involved?" I ask, worriedly.

"Who knows? But I'll find out today. I'm going to set a trap, just like she did."

"She set a trap?" I ask.

"Of course. She knew you were coming over Thursday night. She orchestrated the whole thing so that you'd walk in on us 'having sex' and break it off."

I growl into my pillow. "I can't believe this. I mean, I'm sorry I didn't trust you, but it was just so believable. Plus, having my own doubts only added to it."

"I know, baby. And I'm not actually mad anymore. At first I was angry that you and Annie didn't believe me, but it looked bad, and I'm just relieved that her drugging me explains what you saw."

"Still, I should've known you wouldn't hurt me like that."

"Well, now you know."

"Yeah. So what trap are you going to set up for Jasmine?"

"I'm going to lure her over," he explains. "I'm going to tell her that you and I have broken up and make it seem like I need a shoulder to cry on."

"Meanwhile, I'll be in the background, ready to pounce?"

"Exactly. Only we'll confront her together. As a team."

"Sounds like a great plan."

***

An hour later, I'm in Ben's bedroom waiting for his signal. We'd planned that when he says my name loud and clear as he's talking to Jasmine, that's when I'm to come out. When we told Annie the plan, she said she wanted to be involved, so she's also waiting beside me. The idea is that Ben will get Jasmine onto the sofa, cornering her so she can't run off.

Ben speaks up, "Well, like I said, *Matthew* won't be your problem anymore." Annie and I step out of the bedroom and into the living room. I smirk at Jasmine when she catches my eye. "You see, it won't just be Matt that is your problem. Now, you have to deal with all three of us."

She sits up straighter. "What the fuck?"

"Here's the thing, Jasmine. For drugging me with Rohypnol, you're looking at a decent amount of jail time. Especially if you raped me, which according to Matt, it's looking like you did. This could be really bad for you. Now is the time for you to explain." He crosses his arms over his chest. He's so dominant and intimidating right now with his wide shoulders in that leather jacket and that feral scowl on his face. I try as hard as possible—pun not intended—to distract myself from being so turned on.

Jasmine cowers into the sofa. "Okay," she whispers. "I'll explain everything."

"Is the baby even Ben's?" I ask her, moving over to Ben's right-hand side as Annie shifts to his left.

"No," she replies, ducking her head.

"What?" Ben whispers.

Jasmine sighs and shakes her head. "I lied. I'm sorry. You're not the father."

Ben's arms unfold.

At his crestfallen face, Jasmine's eyes water. "I'm so sorry, Ben."

"You bitch! Why would you do that to him? You made him believe he was going to be a father!" Annie yells at her.

"I know," Jasmine sobs. "I'm sorry. When we were together I met this other guy. I slipped up and had sex with him. You remember those few weeks that I refused to have sex?" She pauses until Ben nods in response. "It was because I felt guilty for cheating on you. And that's how I knew it wasn't yours when I found out I was pregnant. The day after you proposed, the guy, Derek, he asked me to follow him back to San Francisco and I did. Of course, after a few months together, he decided he wasn't ready to be a father and I got kicked out on my ass. I was just so caught up in the money. I needed the money so bad. I'm really sorry, Ben. I'm sorry for getting your hopes up about a daughter. And I'm sorry for causing the both of you such trouble." She directs the last part of her speech to both me and Ben.

After a few quiet moments, I ask, "What money? Who was offering you money?" At this, Jasmine locks her jaw. She fidgets and doesn't meet our eyes.

"Jasmine?" Ben pleads with her softly. "Please just tell me. Did you actually rape me on Thursday night?" She shakes her head and says she just got on top of him for me to see it, just like Ben guessed. "Then, I won't be taking any legal action against you. I promise. But only on the condition that you tell me, right now, who was giving you money? Did someone pay you to do this?" She sobs quietly and then whispers so softly that we can't hear her. "What?" he asks.

"It was Brandon," she whimpers. Annie and I gasp.

Ben frowns deeply. "My dad?"

Jasmine nods. "He called me a while ago and said he'd pay me if I broke the two of you up."

Ben's jaw drops. "What?"

"As horrible as it is, it's true. I'm so sorry. He called me about a month ago and said he'd just found out you had a boyfriend. Said he'd pay me ten grand if I managed to break the two of you up. I needed a place to live and with a baby on the way, I didn't hesitate. I'm sorry. I know this makes me a horrible person. Honestly, your dad doesn't know anything about the drug. That was my own fucked-up idea. I panicked when it seemed like the pregnancy wouldn't do it."

"But this whole lie and manipulation wasn't, was it? That's my dad."

She nods. "He suggested the baby idea. It was just his dumb luck that I actually am pregnant. He said the only reason you'd let me back into your life would be a baby."

"That fucking asshole!" Ben shouts. Stroking his arm, I push my body into his and wrap my arms around his waist. Hugging him to me tightly, I'm pleased beyond belief when Ben hugs me back. "How could he do this to me? To us? He knows how happy I am with you."

I rub his back in comforting strokes. "This must be

why he snatched the phone from your mom and didn't put you on speaker phone. He didn't want Catherine knowing about the whole thing," I say. "I'm so sorry, Ben."

He lifts my head with his thumb under my chin. "Why are you sorry?"

"Because no one should have a father like this. This deceitful and manipulative. He hurt you, and a father should never hurt his son."

"I'm no son of his," Ben growls. "I don't want anything to do with him. How can I ever speak to someone like him ever again? Why would I?"

"I think you need to show him, make him see that no matter what he does, he'll never change who you are and who you love. It's your life, not his."

Ben cradles my face in his hands. "What is the point in telling him? His opinion on anything doesn't mean shit to me now. The fact that he could do this to me has made me lose all respect for him. No, what I'm going to do is tell Mom what he's done. She should know."

"Okay."

"Come with me?"

I smile then kiss him softly. "Of course."

16

BENJAMIN

The discussion with my mother is difficult and then amusing. Catherine Stokes is an astute, resilient woman who is not easily surprised. So when Matt and I visit her and explain everything that happened with Dad, Jasmine, my supposed baby, and the drugging, she goes apeshit. My mother, the conservative, poised, gentle lady that she is, actually goes apeshit. She's yelling and pacing and waving her slender fists in the air. For a moment, I think I'm in shock, but the minute she's up and raving, I start to chuckle. Matt nudges me with his arm, but it only makes it worse. It's when she says, "I'll fucking kill him, that cold-hearted motherfucker!" that I burst out laughing. In her Victorian-styled living room on her nice chaise lounge, I'm bellowing with laughter. She suddenly snaps her head around. "What the fuck is so funny, Benjamin?"

In between chuckles, I finally manage to reply. "I don't… think I… have ever heard you swear! Or seen you yell. Ever. In my whole life!" My words are broken up as I try to gather my breath. After a minute, Matt starts giggling at me and this causes Mom to start laughing too. We all laugh for a moment before she sits down in front of us again.

"Ben, I'm so sorry," she begins. "I'd like to say I'm surprised, but honestly and unfortunately, I'm not. Your father has been acting strangely for a while. Ever since our dinner together."

I nod. "Matt was saying that maybe when he went to the bathroom, he got in contact with Jasmine. And even though he didn't mind me getting my hopes up, he didn't want you speaking to me on the phone that time because I was about to tell you that you guys were going to be grandparents. He obviously wanted to save you from that hurt."

She scoffs. "Or save himself from being found out."

"Yeah."

Mom leans forward and grasps my hand in hers. "I love you, Benjamin, and I'm sorry that your own father tried to sabotage the loving relationship you two have." She smiles at Matt warmly. "I can only thank God that it didn't ruin your chances of happiness. You, Matthew, have made my boy so happy. I can't thank you enough for that."

Matt squeezes my other hand. "He makes me happy

too, Catherine. More than you could ever know. He's my other half. I'm just relieved it was all explained. If it hadn't been for my sister suggesting that Ben get tested for drugs, we would've never known the truth."

"Yes, I suppose you'll be taking legal action?" Mom asks me.

"No." I shake my head as she tilts hers in confusion. "She's explained what happened and why she did it. I just want to forget this whole thing happened. Besides Dad's part in it. That I'll never forgive."

"I don't blame you," she says sadly.

"I love you, Mom. No matter what goes down with me and Dad, I'll always have you in my life."

"Thank you, son." She glances back over to Matt. "Personally, I find that your love is a blessing. Now, not only do I have one son, I have two."

Matt's eyes start to water. "Thank you, Mrs. Stokes." As her eyebrow lifts, he quickly corrects himself. "Thank you, *Catherine*. That means a lot to me."

"You're welcome."

Once we leave the apartment, I change my mind and drive us to Dad's office. The receptionist tries to stop me from just barging through. "Wait! Ah, Mr.… Stokes, Mr. Stokes is on an important phone call!"

"He'll see me!" I bark back to her, pulling Matt along by the hand.

At the sound of the door bursting open, my father stands up without looking. "Grace! What did I tell you! Don't just let someone—" His eyes finally lift and he takes in the sight of us standing in front of him.

With my left hand holding Matt's, I slide the other into my jacket pocket. "Hello, Dad. I'm not just someone, am I? I'm your son. Or at least I was."

"Dr. Walker, I'll have to call you back." Brandon Stokes hangs up his phone and then places his hands on his hips. "Benjamin, why are you barging into my office? And what are you talking about?"

"I'm here to deliver a message," I say, letting go of Matt's hand and stalking forward toward the desk. "You are not to contact either me or Matt ever again. I don't want anything to do with you."

"What?" He seems surprised at my anger.

"I know, Dad. About the deal with Jasmine. How could you? Actually forget it. Whatever fucked-up reason made you decide that it was a good idea, it doesn't matter. I just came here to tell you that I don't want to see you ever again."

"Ben, be reasonable. I just didn't want you with this… boy. I wanted the best for you. I just want you to be happy."

"What made you think that I wasn't?" I shout. He actually jerks in shock. "No one has made me happier or made life more worth living than my Matthew. I love him, and for some reason, he loves me back. I meant what I said. With your actions—calling Jasmine and sabotaging my relationship with him—you've obliterated any ties we had, as well as any chance of a relationship with any future baby I *actually* have!"

Out of the corner of my eye, I see Matt move forward to stand by my side. "Ben?"

Lowering and turning my head to gaze into Matt's eyes, I tell Dad, "One day, Matt and I are going to start a family." Matt's eyes widen and the smile he gives me is so fucking beautiful, it encourages me. I look back to Dad. "You will not have anything to do with our children, do you hear me? Nothing. What you did was wrong on way too many levels."

Dr. Brandon Stokes moves to the front of his desk. "Son, I'm sorry, okay? I'm sorry that I tried to break the two of you up. And I apologize for orchestrating the whole thing. Making you think you were going to be a dad was cruel, but I knew it was the only reason you would even consider allowing Jasmine to re-enter your life."

Taking a deep breath, I ask the only other question I have for him. "She said you didn't, but I want to make sure. Did you supply her the Rohypnol?"

Dad's jaw drops as the skin on his forehead pulls back. "What?"

I nod. "Okay, at least with that reaction, I know you didn't."

His face scrunches up. "Wait! What the fuck? Why are you talking about Rohypnol?"

Matt pipes up beside me. "The girl you had break me and your son up, she drugged him. She mixed it with alcohol and made sure he was out of it in time for me to walk in on them 'fucking.'" Matt hooks his fingers in the air, making quotation marks.

Brandon collapses into a chair in disbelief. "Jasmine drugged you?"

"Yeah," I confirm. "I'm not taking legal action against her because she explained the whole thing and gave me her word that I wouldn't ever have to see her again." Grabbing Matt's hand in mine, I start to lead the way out. "Oh, and FYI, Mom knows everything. You might want to go home before she ruins *all* of your baseball and football memorabilia."

"I don't care about that stuff. Ben?" The anguish in his voice is the only thing that makes me turn around. His eyes are red and watery. "I know you'll never forgive me. I don't blame you. But just so you know, I'm sorry. I never… I know now that I was being completely selfish. I wasn't thinking about you. You're right. There was nothing that made me think you weren't happy. I was only trying to keep my Ben, the way you've always been."

"And now you won't have me at all," I say, shrugging away my hurt. "Your need to confine me to fit your ways has cost you me."

He rubs his eyes roughly. "I know. I'm not asking for your forgiveness. I just want you to know that I'm sorry. That I love you, just as you are."

Nodding stiffly, I grasp Matt's hand and leave Dad's office. Time to go home.

***

Normally, when it comes to Christmas, it's just me and my parents getting together. This year, I spend the day with the twins and Mom comes over for lunch. She and Dad have apparently separated for now. He's renting another apartment closer to work. It's clear that they're still in love, but, like me, Mom is having trouble forgiving him.

"Every time I see or speak to your father, he tells me how sorry he is, how he wishes he could rewind time," she says at the front door as she's leaving. "I know it's only been a few weeks, and you might not ever forgive him for what he did, but you should know that he's genuinely sorry."

"Okay," I say, hugging her close. "I'll take what you're saying on board, but I need more time. Even the thought of seeing him makes me angry still."

"I understand. In time, perhaps we'll both forgive him." She caresses my cheek before she hugs Annie and Matt. "Don't be strangers now, you two. I want to go on another shopping trip."

"Oh yes! That sounds great!" Annie says.

"Brand whore," I murmur quietly, making the twins laugh.

"Bye! And Merry Christmas!" Mom says as she leaves.

"Merry Christmas!" we shout back.

***

That night when we're lying in bed about to make love, I stop Matt from stripping off my shirt.

"What's wrong?" he asks, his blue eyes imploring me to get naked.

"I have another Christmas present for you," I say, pressing him into the bed and standing up. For Christmas I bought both him and Annie a coffeemaker and for Matt a new sketching kit. Annie also got an e-reader from me. Matt bought me a new tool kit that I'd been wanting to buy and Annie bought me the box set of *Frasier*. She also gave me and Matt a voucher for a two-night stay at a luxurious hotel in Manhattan. I felt completely spoiled.

"Oh?" Matt smiles widely. "What is it?"

"Do you remember that sketch of yours I saw the first time you let me look in your sketchbook? And a few weeks ago I wanted a copy of it?" We'd been going through a bunch of Matt's sketches at the time because he'd finally listened to my suggestion of putting his name out there. My boy is skilled and I wanted him to show off his stuff. One of my mom's close friends, who manages an art museum, said she'd have a look at his work. After showcasing a few of his sketches, he now has a couple of commissions that will keep him busy and hopefully help spread the word of his talent.

I see the recognition in his expression. "The phoenix?"

"Yeah," I whisper. "What does the phoenix represent to you?"

"Again?" he asks with a laugh. I nod seriously, which

makes him huff. “For me, it means resurrection, renewal, rebirth, or a new start… those kinds of things.”

“I agree,” I say. “When I met you, my life changed completely. I realized things about myself that I never knew.”

“Like the fact that you’re into guys?” he quips.

“Like the fact that I could love someone as strongly as I love you.” His smile is shy. Slowly, I peel my shirt off. “In many ways, you gave me a new life, Matt. It’s because of you that I now feel reborn. I’m a better boyfriend and a better person than I thought I could ever be. I think it’s only right that your beautiful sketch is immortalized. And what better place to have it than on my skin?” Keeping my eyes on him, I slowly turn around so he can see my back. With my head over my shoulder, I watch as Matt gasps and jumps off the bed. Standing behind me now, he’s gazing at my new tattoo in awe.

It took a few sessions over the last few weeks to have it completed. Although I told Matt I was getting new ink on my back, it has been the ultimate challenge keeping it from him and not allowing him to see it. A few weeks ago, I’d asked for a copy of his beautiful drawing of a phoenix with its wings spread and flames under and around it. Immediately I knew that was what I wanted to replace my tattoo of the Grim Reaper. Luckily, when I went to a tattoo parlor and showed my boy’s sketch to an artist, he said it wouldn’t be a problem. Plus, with all of the colorful shading, it is absolutely beautiful and I love it. It is a tattoo I can now take pride in wearing. The wings are shaded with the gay pride colors, the flames are orange, yellow and red, and the phoenix is a light gray. In black ink, "Matthew" is written in a cursive font where the mythical bird's heart would be.

"Ben," he whispers.

"You like?"

"I absolutely love it. It is so beautiful."

"Almost as beautiful as you."

His eyes finally leave my back to meet with mine. Dropping to the floor on one knee, he blurts out, "Will you marry me?"

Blinking in shock for a moment, eventually I answer. "I'm sorry, I just thought I would be the one to ask you. Yes, yes I will marry you."

With a leap, he jumps into my arms and I catch him. Holding him close, I tell him how much I love him.

"Show me how much you love me?" he asks.

"With pleasure." Placing him back down on the bed, I spread his legs and lie down in between them. Pressing my lips over his belly button, I slowly make my way up his body until I reach his lips. Like usual, the passion becomes too much and we can't help ourselves. Grinding our groins together, we make out until we can't wait any longer.

"Get inside me," Matt moans.

Over the last few weeks, we've been broadening our horizons in the bedroom. Tonight I want to use the blindfold again as well as something new. Jumping up, I open the drawer and tell him to close his eyes. When he does, I tie the blindfold over them with a nice, firm grip. He smiles at me.

"I love your smile, baby," I whisper against his mouth, kissing him softly. "Tonight, I want to try something new."

"What?"

"Tsk, tsk, tsk. Be patient." He sighs when I start to rub his nipples. Giving them each a lick, I tell him that I have a new toy. "They're nipple clamps. I'm going to put them on, but just tell me if they hurt too much and I'll loosen them, okay?"

"Okay."

Playing with his nipples until they're erect, I pinch and then clamp them. His only response is a drawn-out groan. The black clamps that I bought each have a feather on the other end. "Oh, Matt. They look beautiful on you."

"Yeah?"

"Yes. How do they feel?"

"They sting a bit, but it's just a tugging sensation. I'm okay."

"Good boy."

Stroking my hands all over his chest, I do this for a few moments, and every once in a while I flick or tug on the clamps. Each time I do this, Matt gives me a sexy groan. Eventually, I open my mouth and take his dick inside. "Ah! Ben!" he moans. Bobbing my head up and down with a fast pace, I get him good and hard. His cock is so beautiful when it's this hard, so erect and swollen.

While my mouth pays it much attention, I get him ready for me and tease his nipples. When I've been pumping three of my fingers inside him for a while and he's ready for me, he's a complete mess. I love it. He's desperate for me now, so desperate for an orgasm that he's pleading with me.

"What do you want, baby?" I make sure to ask him this once I have his legs in my hands and my cock at his hole.

"You!"

"Okay." Pushing forward swiftly, I plunge inside of him all the way.

"Fuck, yes!" He starts whimpering now as he spreads his legs farther apart. When I rest my hands on the bed on either side of him, he pushes the heels of his feet into my back and wraps his hands around my arms.

I growl. "That's it, baby. Hold on tight." Aware that I'm not going to last long inside of him, I make the next few minutes count. As I'm pounding into him, my lips find his. He kisses me frantically, causing me to falter. My boy is always so hungry for me. I absolutely love it. Taking his bottom lip with my teeth, I nibble and suck on it before sliding my tongue into his mouth. Matt moans deeply, sucking on my tongue. When we break apart for air, his breathing has changed and I know he's about to come. Leaning up onto my knees, I continue thrusting my hips forward as I grasp both nipple clamps and remove their biting grip. Matt yells out. I take his cock in hand and jerk him off.

"Oh God, oh God, oh God!" His chanting makes me grin widely. That is, until his orgasm tightens his body's grip on my cock. Moaning, I buck into him over and over until I'm coming deep inside of him. Matt gasps then groans in pleasure. "Yeah," he whispers. "Fuck me, Ben. Fill me."

"Shit, baby." My hips jerk a couple more times, and then I'm done. Rolling us onto our sides, I remove the blindfold and stare into his eyes. "I love you, Matthew Price."

"I love you too, Benjamin Stokes."

"So," I say, as we try to gather our breath, "am I going to be Benjamin Price soon?"

He blinks. "I don't know. I mean, would you prefer me to be Matthew Stokes?"

"I do love the sound of it," I admit. "But I don't mind. If you want to keep your name, that's fine."

"I like the idea of taking your name. Plus, even though Annie will take some guy's surname sometime down the track, with all of my cousins, there are enough Prices in the world."

"Hmm, Benjamin and Matthew Stokes. I really like the sound of it."

Matt yawns. "Has a nice ring to it."

"Speaking of rings," I start, eager to put a ring on his finger.

"We'll go looking tomorrow," he says. "Post-holiday sales."

"Okay." I yawn. "Come on, have a shower with me."

"I'm too tired."

"Come on," I coax him, pulling on his arm. In the shower, neither of us have much energy, so we make quick work of cleaning ourselves then we're hopping back out. Drying our bodies and sliding back into bed naked, it's when I have my arms tightly wrapped around him that I say, "You're mine. Mine all mine, *fiancé*."

He chuckles and kisses me on the lips. "Still my possessive prick, I see."

I kiss his nose. "And you're still my cocky fucker."

"Always."

Epilogue

MATTHEW

Twenty years later

Placing portions of scrambled eggs on everyone's pieces of toast, I yell, "Breakfast!"

Loud, thumping footsteps can be heard as everyone races down the stairs and toward me in the kitchen. Marie and Masen arrive first. Sliding into their chairs, they barely avoid knocking their hot drinks over. My love walks in last. Strutting over to me, he gives me a chaste kiss and says, "Morning, baby." With a few wrinkles on either side of his eyes and silver streaks in his hair, to me, Ben is hotter than ever.

I moan against his mouth. "Hey, hotstuff."

"Papa!" Masen groans. "I'm trying to eat."

Turning around and joining our seventeen-year-old twins, Ben and I take our seats. Two years after I proposed to Ben, Annie delivered our baby twins. She donated an egg, which we had Ben's sperm inseminated into, and she was our surrogate. *Best sister in the world goes to Annie Price.* Marie was named after our mother and Masen was Ben's pop's name. Our teenagers are a delightful mix of our genes. Both with dark brown hair and blue eyes, their skin tone is darker than mine and lighter than Ben's.

Working as hard as Ben and I do, it's nice to enjoy a simple family breakfast before everyone heads off to school or work for the day. About ten years ago, Ian retired and Ben bought him out, making him the sole owner of Stokes Repairs. Ever since I completed the first two artwork commissions, my art career skyrocketed. When the twins were babies, I had commissions left, right, and center. I had to reel it in though. Until a few years ago, I wouldn't allow myself a heavy work schedule, but as the kids grow up and Ben gets more help at the garage, I challenge myself a little more each time.

"Sorry, Mase," I say, bringing myself back to the here and now. "I won't talk about how sexy your dad is."

"Yeah, good. Don't do that," Marie pipes up, smirking at me.

Ben laughs. "I'm sort of looking forward to when they go off to college," he muses.

"Dad!" Marie warns.

I join in with the teasing. "So much free time."

"Papa!" Masen whines.

After everyone's laughter settles down and we're eating, we fill each other in on what we have planned for the day. Marie tells us that she and Masen are going over to their nan and pop's after school. Fortunately, a year after the whole Jasmine incident, Ben and his dad started talking again. By the time our kids arrived, they were closer than ever before. I'm glad they were able to patch things up between them, because with my parents having passed away many years ago now, I'm pleased that our kids have grown up with grandparents.

Placing my coffee mug down, I say, "Aunt Annie and Uncle Sam are coming for dinner on Friday night."

"Cool!" they say in unison.

Funnily enough, when Annie was pregnant with our kids, she met Sam. Two years later, they were married and Annie gave birth to their son, James, who was named after our father. When the twins were six and James was three, Annie had her daughter Isla. Ben and I try to plan dinner dates with them at least a few times a month as all the kids are close.

Marie finishes her food and sits back. "Isla will be twelve soon."

"She will," I agree. "Any idea what we should get her?"

"Nope."

"What about a Barbie doll?" Masen asks.

Marie scowls. "She's twelve."

He shrugs. "Makeup?"

"She's twelve," she repeats.

"Oh, whatever. Don't ask for my help then."

"I didn't."

Masen groans loudly in frustration and looks to us for help. Marie simply smirks.

I catch Ben's eye as he looks at me. "What?" I ask.

He strokes my cheek and leans in for a quick kiss. "I love you, baby. More than ever before." This time, the twins remain silent with identical smiles.

"Me too," I whisper. "And our love will only continue to grow."

"Forever?" he asks.

"Forever."

Acknowledgements

First and foremost, to Becky, Justine, Kristin, Kolleen, and Donna at Hot Tree Publishing, along with the women who beta read my story. Thank you so much for all of your help with this book. Your support and assistance has allowed me to share Matt and Ben's story with pride. I'll be forever grateful for your acceptance, guidance, and tender care of this book.

To my mum and dad, Maria and Jon Andrews, your consistent love and support through life has made me the person I am today. I'm so lucky to have parents such as yourselves. I love you with all of my heart.

My brother, Jason, thanks for supporting me with my writing and cheers for making me and buying me coffee as often as you do.

My cousin Brielle, thank you for bouncing back so many ideas for my stories. I love our movie days together, and I promise if any of my books ever become a movie (ha-ha) I'll do all I can to get you in it :P

I'd like to give a shout-out to my friends for their love and support: Feliece, Ruby, Kate, Lisa, Laura, Sophie, Ingrid, Nadia, and Catherine.

Family, friends, work colleagues, and acquaintances who have put up with my pestering ways to convert you into book lovers, thank you for your patience and support.

To the wonderful people I met through FanFiction, thank you! This is where I first started reading m/m romance and fell in love with many stories. I loved them so much that I started writing my own as well.

To the authors who inspired me to write including; Stephenie Meyer, Jodi Piccoult, James Patterson, and my two favourites, Nalini Singh and J.R. Ward, thank you! With your wonderful words, you continue to take me to places that allow my imagination to run free.

Finally, to you, my wonderful readers, thank you so much for purchasing this book. I hope you enjoyed Matt and Ben's love story, *Forever You*. I know I loved writing it.

- L. N. A

Trade Me Collection

Trade me is a Hot Tree Publishing exclusive genre-linked collection of novellas. Stories are all hot gay m/m romances with a strong HEA and have at least one of the lead characters having a sexy trade.

Be sure to look out for monthly releases in this collection.

Are you an author?

Our Trade Me collection is currently open for submissions. No deadline. Check out our website WWW.HOTTREEPUBLISHING.COM for submission information.

Printed in Australia
AUOC01n0643151116
280522AU00001B/1/P

9 781925 448436